SECRET OF CERES BOOK 3

EARNEST

STELLA WILLIAMS

Earnest: Secret of Ceres Book 3

Ebook ISBN: 978-1-7347301-2-8
Print ISBN: 978-1-7347301-3-5

Editing
Raw Book Editing
www.rawbookediting.com

Book Cover Design
RebeccaCovers

Published by
Serpentine Creative LLC
www.serpentinecreative.com
PO Box 3582
Pasco, WA 99302

For all the women who exemplify Black Girl Magic

Spirits

Ruling Three poured over the paperwork in front of him, doing his best to avoid thinking about what would happen when Maximus returned his call. Disrayan had escaped; Ruling Three needed a replacement who was just as powerful if not more powerful all without drawing suspicion to himself. It would be his last dealing with the Vampire, now his original plan was back on track. He set his pen on his desk and rubbed his eyes. He'd been staring at the paperwork for hours, and nothing about them had changed. He had officially signed his agreement to participate in the reelection of Ruling Council Members. Now, it was time to venture out amongst the masses and get his hands dirty.

He needed to ensure they remained on his side, so when push came to shove no one would question his right to sole leadership of Ceres. A glance out the window behind his desk gave him a moment of pause. The usually clear purple sky now hung a low greenish gray fog, blocking out the view of the merchant stalls below. His first order of business once he was reelected was to purge all those who acted against him. Then he could fix the Barrier for good.

Ruling Three pushed away from his desk and left his office. He waved away the two Security Force Officers on his detail.

"I don't need you following me to the restroom," he scoffed when they didn't immediately leave his side.

The two guards eyed each other before repositioning themselves in front of his office door. Ruling Three may not be Ruling Council anymore, but Commander Mars insisted due to the contentious state of things he remain guarded at all times. Pesky man would be one of the first to go with the rest of his meddlesome Holier Than Thou family.

He headed in the direction of the restroom, but once out of sight of the guards, he changed course, heading up the stairs to the control room for the Barrier. He'd timed his trip perfectly to be between shifts. Even with the increased watch after the Barrier Incident, Ruling Three ensured there was always a short window when he could augment the Barrier without anyone else's knowledge.

Letting his energy flow, he channeled it into the crystal that balanced the energy necessary to maintain the Barrier. First, a little give, then a little take. Ruling Three siphoned the energy he needed until he felt it begin to waver. He didn't want to destabilize the Barrier, but drawing on its energy to boost his own had become an addiction of sorts. He'd made that mistake once, and while it had eventually worked in his favor, he couldn't risk letting his greed be the death of him and his dreams for Ceres.

He cut himself off and took a step back. The usual high he received from the mass of energy wasn't giving him the same boost as it usually did. Something he'd been noticing since the incident. The more he tried to draw, the less of a high he felt. Ruling Three didn't have time to dwell on the matter. He needed to make it back before anyone got suspicious. He made a pit stop in the restroom and smiled when he saw his reflection in the mirror. The few small wrinkles that had appeared on his forehead and at the crease of his eyes were barely visible, and the few grey hairs that had sprouted over the last week were nowhere to be found.

The people were under the impression he used his own energy and human aging treatments to maintain his good looks. Little did they know, it was the Barrier's energy that kept him looking and feeling so young. Exiting the bathroom, he nearly ran into Commander Mars. The man stood like an imposing wall of muscle right in Ruling Three's way.

"Bartholomew, I assigned you a guard for your own protection."

Despite the appearance of being younger, Ruling Three and Commander Mars were the same age. Ruling Three straightened his posture and looked down his nose at Commander Mars. At least, as best he could when up against a man several inches taller than he. Before ascending to his position on the Council and gaining access to the balancing crystal, Ruling Three would have appeared shrunken and grey in comparison to the massive man before him. Ruling Three's family just didn't have the same warrior genes. Something Commander Mars had flaunted ruthlessly during training in their younger years.

"You may address me as Ruling Three, as I am surely without threat of not being reelected."

Commander Mars didn't so much as move a muscle. No matter how much status Ruling Three achieved, Mars always held an air of superiority that struck the deepest of nerves with Ruling Three. He couldn't wait to complete his plans and finally take Mars down several pegs.

"Protocol dictates you resume your given name until after elections, regardless of your confidence in reelection. Now, you will not attempt to command my men in the future if you wish to survive until the elections."

"Is that a threat?"

"Just an assessment of the situation. You've already been knocked on your ass twice. A man of your age and comportment might not so easily regain their footing the next time."

Ruling Three bristled at the dig, but the small group of Aura observing the scene meant he needed to play his role.

"Your concern for my wellbeing is much appreciated. I'm glad to have your support this election season, Commander."

Ruling Three made his way out of the Meeting House with his new guard in tow. A smile on his face, he greeted the waiting masses, clasping hands and commiserating with those who'd lost their homes during the Barrier Incident.

"You have my family's support, Ruling Three."

"We love you, Ruling Three."

"Can you bless our child, Ruling Three?"

The people of Ceres were right where he wanted them. In complete and utter awe of him.

.....

A low fog drifted across the landscape, swirling around the tombstones. The low sun casting shadows that seemed poised to spring to life. The air thick and musty despite the soft breeze rustling the leaves of the large tree just a few feet from where Enora Circinus settled in to appease the restless spirits. Cross-legged, eyes closed, the usual calm of the Langsmith cemetery was broken.

This wasn't her usual place. Enora preferred the protection and peace provided by the Aura's resting place. She didn't have the time today to go deep into the cemetery. Her current position was only a few rows of tombs from the access road where she had parked. The spirits didn't seem pleased with her location choice either. The waves of energy pricked her skin like tiny ant bites. Even the grass beneath her felt extra prickly through her pants.

Help me...

Enora refused to open her eyes. Instead, concentrating on balancing the tumultuous energy the newly laid bodies created. The two women had been found drained of all blood, riddled with bite marks. Vampires in Langsmith were getting bolder and more violent, and didn't bode well for the supernatural balance of the town.

"Where did they attack you?"

Help me...

"I will help you, but first, I need you to help me. Where did they take you?"

Her question was met with silence at first. Then her whole body lurched forward as the spirit rushed her, melding with Enora's energy. Enora rocked back and forth as flashes of the young woman partying at Club Obelisk turned into the same girl stumbling through a back alley. *She'd been drugged.*

That information wasn't entirely new. The women Enora's

friends had helped save all shared a similar tale. They'd gone out to have fun, either to a house party or club, only to be drugged and held as Vampire hostages. Enora felt the spirit getting more agitated as the visions progressed. Anxiety built in her chest; her throat began to close off. Unable to properly breath, darkness began to close in, her own vision fading to black as the visions got more intense and more real. She could feel the cool metal of handcuffs on her wrists. Thick cigar smoke burned her nose and choked her even more.

"Enough!" Enora barked, forcing her energy to separate from the spirit before she herself was dragged into the land of the dead. She wanted to help this spirit move on; she needed the information the spirit had to help save others. It was part of her job, but that didn't mean Enora was willing to die to do so.

As a Medical Examiner for Langsmith County and a Security Force Officer, Enora worked on the front lines of shielding the supernatural from the human world. She was the one who had to explain away the bite marks as animal bites, then make sure she didn't name any animals common amongst the area's Shifters. The last thing they needed was for humans to go hunting the killer creature and injure yet another innocent, or worse, discover the existence of supernaturals, and more specifically, the Aura in Langsmith.

Help Me

The only thing more frustrating than covering for the Vampires was dealing with the spirits of their victims. Their deaths were often traumatic, and thus, moving into the afterlife was harder for them. Enora could just leave them to haunt the cemetery, but she couldn't sit idly by when she had the knowledge to help them find some peace in death. Even when they tried to kill her with their impatience. She stretched a little before settling back in to her sitting position and closing her eyes once more. Letting her energy swell, she felt for the thinning of veil between the living and the afterlife. It was a skill few knew she possessed. The Aura had outlawed most of the knowledge involving communing with the afterlife. It was dark energy work. The same dark energy that led them to be demonized and exiled to Ceres in the first place.

"Follow my energy to the light."

Enora let her energy expand once more. Weaving through the

rows of headstones like the lighted walkways on planes. She waited for the candle in front of her to extinguish. It was linked to the opening she created in the veil. Once the spirit passed through, the opening would seal behind it and the flame would die out.

Open Season

Enora's brows furrowed. She wasn't sure if the spirit was speaking gibberish or trying to give her a clue as to where her abductors had taken her. The longer spirits lingered in limbo, the more disoriented they became. It was one of the reasons Enora came to them so soon after they were buried. The sooner she reached them, the easier to talk them through to the other side.

"What?"

Cabin Fever

A stiff wind blew, and Enora pulled her coat tighter around her shoulders. She could sense another presence moving closer. She concentrated harder on guiding the woman's spirit to the other side. Yet, the woman didn't seem to want to follow. Enora felt the spirit pressing in closer, trying to merge again, but she blocked her out. Enora was not doing that again.

Over the river and through the woods

"There is no river in Langsmith," Enora muttered more to herself than the spirit.

Over the River!

"Just follow my energy to the other side before it's too late."

In her frustration, Enora's eyes fluttered open.

Enora felt a slight warmth on her shoulder, the whisper of a touch before a rush of energy let her know the spirit had crossed. Her shoulders relaxed, and she opened her eyes again. The breeze still moved the trees, but the whisper of leaves was all that was left on the night air. Her job here was done. She gathered her blanket and candle before heading through the rows of tombstones to the road where her car was parked.

Once inside, she cranked her heater on high and dug into her purse for her phone. It was 11:30 at night. She was exhausted, but the thought of going home to a cold empty bed just wasn't appealing. Biting her lip, she scrolled through her contacts until she found the number she was looking for.

E: You up?
J: For You? Always.

Enora ignored the flutter of her heart. Jaquis Andromeda wasn't the relationship type. That was why she chose him for nights like these. They had chemistry in bed, and she didn't have to worry about the pressure of letting someone into her life. At least, that was the excuse she was giving for her inability to stay away from her best friend's brother. There were countless reasons she should stop their arrangement.

E: 10 minutes
J: I'll be there in 5

Shaking her head, Enora tossed her phone to the side and drove off. He would most likely already be at her door when she arrived.

.....

Jaquis Andromeda sat back in his chair. A lazy smile curved his full lips and accentuated his strong jaw and cheek bones. He meant for the smile to be disarming, to put at ease the frustrating man in front of him.

"I assure you; The Resistance only wants what is best for the Aura," Jaq said.

"If that was true, why are you so reckless in your use of energy knowledge? How can you say you are for the people when half of the missing girls have been tied to your little rebellion?"

Jaquis sat up. It was true. Most of the Aura who had been taken by rogue Vampires had in fact been tied to The Resistance. Was it a coincidence? Maybe, maybe not. The answer to that question was one he was active in solving.

"The Resistance is committed to the freedom of the Aura. Our members are encouraged to be true to themselves, not to shy away from their abilities or their history. I can't say The Resistance hasn't been targeted because of this. What I can say is we are taking every precaution to ensure the safety of our members."

The man stared Jaq down a moment longer before scribbling his name on the sign-up sheet in front of Jaq.

"Well, the Ruling Council has led us into this hole. What's the harm in trying something new?"

The man turned away, and a young woman approached the table. A blush crept into her pale cheeks as she scrawled her name below the man's.

"I, I. My friend said..." She was so flustered she couldn't get her words out.

Jaq's gaze flickered to the newest initiate into The Resistance. A Shifter teen by the name of Sarah, who was generally quiet and spent most of her time in a corner observing. Most of the time, Jaq would forget she was in the room. At least until now. With a spark in her eye, Sarah moved closer to the table, eyes trained on the girl in front of Jaq.

"It's okay to be nervous about joining. Come on, I'll show you around," Sarah said sweetly, pulling the girl away.

Jaq sighed and stood from the table. He usually left this part of recruitment to others, but today, he'd needed to see firsthand what his second in command had raved about. Membership of The Resistance was in fact exploding thanks to the implosion of the Ruling Council and the unrest caused by the Barrier Incident.

It was hard to believe it had already been a month since he'd gotten Farrah's call. The gate had been closed, people were panicked that something had happened, and it turned out their fears were warranted. The gate was shut because the Barrier protecting Ceres had nearly collapsed in on itself. No one had lost their lives, but many had lost their homes within Ceres. So much for being a sanctuary for the Aura. It seemed more and more like a death trap. The Barrier still hadn't recovered from the incident. If Jaq's sources were correct, things were getting worse.

Add to that, the turmoil within the Ruling Council, his cousin Hendrex being removed as Ruling Four, and a call for emergency reelections. Ceres was falling and the political structure that could have eased the fears of the people was no longer available. Ceres was a sham, and the human world was the only option for the continued survival for the Aura people. If only they would let go of their ingrained prejudice and fear of the unknown. The human world was so much more vast and accepting now than it had been when Ceres was created. That didn't mean their fears were completely unfounded.

Jaq would be an idiot not to acknowledge the Vampire threat here in Langsmith. Like the man had rudely pointed out in his questioning of The Resistance, the Aura were targets. As the leader of The Resistance, in order to keep his goal of Aura freedom viable, the threat needed to be neutralized. Jaq made his way outside. He needed some air to clear his head before going back in to face all the questions. The problem with being the leader was everyone expected you to have answers to everything.

"Running from responsibility already?"

Jaq nearly jumped at the unexpected company. He forced a smile before turning to his cousin.

"Says the man who was willing to let his own brother face the gallows, instead of facing his ex-lover," Jaq replied.

Mack punched Jaq in the shoulder.

"I didn't, though, not like it mattered."

"Oh, it mattered, just wasn't the outcome you wanted."

"Yeah, but it's working out for you to have the Council disbanded. You could barely handle the like, ten people in your group before. How are you going to keep up with this lot?"

Jaq scowled at Mack.

"You're lucky you are my cousin. Don't worry about what I've got going. Shouldn't you be home with Rye anyway? She didn't look so hot yesterday after the hearing."

Mack's cocky grin slid from his face at the mention of his complicated partner.

"She's resting, but I wanted to get everyone together to discuss some new developments."

Jaq sighed. Mack was right about one thing. Jaq was tired of the politics. First, with the Aura traffickers, then the Barrier Incident, and now, the Ruling Council. It was a lot to keep track of, and it seriously cramped his style. Jaq couldn't focus on the main goal of The Resistance without clearing this other mess up first.

"I'm down to bail on the rest of this. My peeps have it handled."

"We'll have to wait until tomorrow. Donovan is busting a monster house right now, and Xander hasn't gotten back to me yet," Mack said.

"Works for me either way," Jaq replied, even though he had been itching for an excuse to exit stage left on the dramatics inside.

"Good, I'll hit you up with more details later, but I've got to get back before Rye wakes. Wouldn't want to poke the bear so soon after she forgave me."

Jaq laughed.

"Just wait 'til I tell her you called her a bear," Jaq said before heading back inside.

The crowd had thinned a little, but not by much. Sarah was in the corner chatting with the pale girl from earlier, and someone had filled in his spot at the table. He wasn't needed for this event, other than to show his face and make sure people were well aware who was in charge here. Jaq stood in an empty corner of the room watching as people mixed, mingled, and argued Aura politics. He'd spent so much of his life avoiding the legacy of leadership in his family and here he was presiding over his own group of not just Aura but humans, Shifters, Vampires, and other supernaturals who weren't satisfied with the status quo. They weren't rogues per se, and they weren't entirely against the structure of their perspective cultures, but hiding their true identities from the world at large didn't sit right with any of them.

Jaq's phone buzzed in his pocket. He almost ignored it, thinking it was just Mack with information about the meeting tomorrow night. Jaq smiled at his phone. He hadn't been sure Enora would want to see him again. Especially, so soon after their last encounter. After a quick back-and-forth, Jaq tucked his phone in his pocket and signaled to Jasmine he was leaving. He was a few blocks from Enora's condo; he would not keep her waiting. Enora was the only bright spot in his life. He'd crushed on her for years, and now was his chance to get what he wanted. Enora in his life for good. All he had to do was play along with her insistence they keep things light until she realized she wanted him just as much as he wanted her.

.....

"I see movement in the south window."

Donovan frowned as the message relayed over his comm. He

signaled the others to halt. So much for being able to sneak in, grab the hostages, and get out. Of course, he knew even the best intel could have pitfalls, but that didn't stop him from cursing Jaq in his head. Jaq had assured him the three suspects wouldn't be at the house that evening.

"Alright, you guys hold tight, and we'll breach from the front."

With the wave of his hand, they were on the move. Donovan thought about how pissed Farrah was going to be that he'd done this mission without her. This was the type of thing she would love to do as a distraction, not just the preparation from their binding ceremony, but also the politics of Ceres.

As it stood, this operation was illegal. The Security Force was in a state of limbo until the Council elections. Without the Ruling Four in place, it was the Security Force's job to maintain the status quo, not to poke the bear. Which was what Donovan was doing. Poking a giant fucking bear, right in the eyeball.

All riled up, Donovan chose not to go for subtlety. He kicked the door in with a loud bang. The three young Vampires inside rushed forward in full attack mode. Donovan backed down the porch, drawing them out into the open. The Aura strike force swooped in. Stunning the Vampires with a direct shot of energy. It was enough to subdue them and take them for questioning later.

Donovan almost followed them to the car. Interrogation was his strong suit, but he needed to clear the house. Make sure there were no further threats and save a few unlucky souls in the process. He just hoped the rest of their intel was correct and the four missing women were still there in Monster House Location six.

"This place is a little less run down than the others," Hector said coming up beside Donovan.

Donovan had noticed as well. The cabin was sparsely furnished but otherwise well-cared for. It looked like a home fit for a single hunter, or maybe an outdoorsy couple. Definitely not like the other monster houses they had come across. Those had been so rundown it was a miracle they were even still standing.

"Let's just get this over with, the sooner we clear this place, the sooner we can get out of harm's way."

Hector nodded, and Donovan felt the shift of his energy as it expanded and threaded throughout the small space. Hector was a tracker and could sense out others' energies within a certain radius. It came in handy on jobs like this one. Tracking the Vampire lairs used to traffic blood slaves to the wealthy amongst them.

It didn't take long for Hector to give the all clear for the main floor. If this house of horrors was anything like the last, there would be a basement where they held the hostages. They checked every door but didn't find another single soul.

"Guess it was bad intel or they already moved whoever they were holding," Hector said.

Donovan shook his head, not ready to give up.

"I want this place turned upside down. Not a single nook or cranny left unturned. They know they have been targeted, maybe they are getting smarter about hiding things."

There were a few grumbles from the men, but they carried out Donovan's direction as ordered. Donovan's phone buzzed in his pocket, and he smiled when he saw Farrah's face on the screen. He didn't answer the call but sent her a text saying they were still searching the scene before returning to his job. She would be pissed he didn't answer, but Donovan would temper her anger with details about everything later. He couldn't blame Farrah for being upset either. If anyone tried to keep him from an investigation he was as invested in as Farrah was with this one, he would have knocked them out and continued on anyway.

Donovan reached the third bedroom in the hall. He couldn't shake the feeling they were missing something here. He pushed around the furniture, stomped on the floor, looking for any sign of a hidden door or passage. With the main room cleared, he moved on to the closet. It was empty, except for a couple of wire hangars and an uncovered bulb hanging from the ceiling. He reached to tug the pull chain, and as soon as the bulb switched on, a panel popped free from the back of the closet.

"I've found something, third room closet," he used his comm to alert the others before pulling the hatch open.

It was dark on the other side of the door, but a slight breeze told him there was a lot more than just a small crawl space beyond the darkness. He pulled out a flashlight and flicked it on. Shining his light into the doorway, there weren't any stairs, just a gaping hole in the ground. He flashed his light down the hole, and there was movement below. Everywhere his flashlight touched, fleeting movement could be seen scurrying away.

"What do we have?" Hector said from behind Donovan.

"We need a ladder," he replied.

Hector moved forward and let out a long slow whistle at the depth of the hole.

"I don't think a ladder is going to cut it."

Donovan took stock of the hole again. Even if they could get a ladder long enough to reach the bottom, they couldn't fit it into the closet. There had to be another way.

"Hello down there, we are here to save you. Can you tell us how they got you down there?"

Donovan frowned at Hector as he yelled into the hole. Before he could rip into Hector for further scaring whatever or whoever was below, a weak childlike voice came from below.

"They drop food and water in a bucket tied to a rope, but when they come to take one of us, it's through the door. There is a tunnel that leads here."

Hector smirked at Donovan before using the comms to have the others search around the perimeter for some sort of storm shelter or covered entrance. It didn't take long for the comms to crackle with news an old storm shelter entrance was found just a few feet outside of the clearing on the north side of the house.

"Just stay calm, we're coming to get you," Donovan shouted.

Excited and scared murmurs came from the hole. Donovan couldn't make out just how many there were. Their frightened energy was too overwhelming for him to even try to get a count.

"I think we may need to arrange for a larger transport. It sounds like there is more than the five we were anticipating," Hector said.

Donovan nodded and smiled at his partner as he pulled out his phone to call Farrah. Of course, Hector was right. They had only banked on there being a few needing to be saved. After the original bust of over fourteen women, the Vampires had kept fewer hostages in each location. Taking the opportunity to include Farrah was a good idea in terms of ensuring the women below felt comfortable and safe, but also gave him points with his future bride.

"Hey, Love. We're going to need your help after all."

"Already on my way," Farrah said with a chuckle.

Donovan shook his head and hung up. Out of the corner of his eye, he could see movement in the tree line. His guard went up until he recognized one of his team leading a small group of women into the clearing.

"This is just the few who were willing to go; there are more that may need more convincing they are safe," Donovan's teammate informed him.

"Farrah and Zarovia will be here soon. They may be of more help with the others. For now, let's get these women in a more secure area in case more vampires show before they do."

Farrah pulled up with Zarovia in a non-descript white passenger van within 30 minutes.

"Do I even want to know how you got a van on such short notice?"

Farrah strode over and wrapped her arms around his neck.

"Do you really want to know?"

Donovan shook his head before kissing her and pulling away.

"As long as you didn't steal it, it doesn't matter."

"Good, because it's a loaner from the school where I work," Zarovia chimed in.

Donovan smiled at Farrah's friend and waved.

"Nice to see you, Zazzie."

"I'd say likewise but given the circumstances." Zazzie nodded toward the other side of the clearing where a group of women huddled looking frightened and uncertain.

Zazzie hopped out of the van and headed toward the group, calming energy radiated from her strong enough to almost lull Donovan to sleep. He was just about to ask her to tone it down when a wave of energy hit Donovan like a speeding train. He fell to the ground as it raked over his skin like rusty nails. The pain and energy overloaded his system, and no amount of shielding seemed to be of any use. His vision blurred and then went black.

Rush

Enora gasped for air as her body came back to reality. Her head pounded like a jackhammer on concrete.

"I wish I could say the sex was that good, but I don't think an orgasm did this," Jaq said beside her.

She whirled on him, which was a big mistake. The sudden movement made the pounding in her head worse, and her stomach lurched. Good thing, she hadn't eaten in a while, otherwise, she would have puked all over him. Jaq caught her in his arms and guided her head to his chest.

"I don't need you to take care of me."

"Let's just lie here until we both can shake whatever the fuck just happened."

"It could be a gas leak. We should get out of the house."

"Case in point, you are the smartest woman I know, but even I know if it was a gas leak, we'd both be dead, instead of talking right now. The sun is up. We passed out when it was dark."

Jaq's hand rubbed along her spine as Enora reached into herself, pulling on her energy to give her strength, but only succeeded in causing herself more panic. Her energy was gone, depleted to the point she was basically Auraless.

She forced herself up, regardless of the pounding of her head and the weakness in her body. Something was wrong.

"Get up!" she barked at Jaq.

He groaned and followed her out of bed. She bit her lip at the sight of his chiseled abs and thick manhood bobbing aimlessly between his legs. If only his personality matched all the man of his body. Then maybe, she could take his affection serious. She took a deep breath and closed her eyes, seeking out his energy. Hers was weak, but there was still enough that she should be able to detect his.

"What are you doing?" Jaq snapped.

Her eyes flew open, and she blushed. She had her rules, and he had his. Jaq was not a fan of energy sharing. He'd made that clear to her their first sober night together. She couldn't blame him. He was from a powerful Aura family. Energy sharing was just as intimate for some as sharing their bodies. Jaq was one of those people.

"Sorry, I just. My energy is super low. I just wanted to see if you were effected the same."

"You could have just asked," he said sliding on his jeans.

She waited for him to continue, and when he didn't, she turned to her drawers to pull out her own clothes.

"Well, I guess someone as powerful as an Andromeda wouldn't need to worry about energy levels," she spat, slamming her drawer closed before she stormed into the bathroom to shower.

She turned on the spray and stepped in with it still cold. Her body still felt groggy and out of whack. She hoped the cool spray would perk her up a bit. It did, and so did Jaq's hands as they wrapped around her waist and pulled her out of the shower. His lips crashed against hers, and she melted into his embrace. She pulled away and smirked at the imprint of her wet boobs against his cotton shirt.

"I feel different too. Something definitely happened last night, and it can't be anything good," Jaq said.

Enora looked into his eyes and cupped his face with her hands. She allowed a rare moment of emotional intimacy between them. Letting him find comfort in her eyes and in her embrace. Then, she dropped her hands and got back in the shower.

"I'll call you." She dismissed him.

Jaq hesitated a moment before turning to leave. It was getting harder and harder each time to dismiss him. Enora didn't want there to be an emotional attachment between them. There were too many complications for them to be together as more than just occasional bed buddies. To take her mind off of Jaq, Enora began a body scan as she washed herself of last night's escapades. She was a little sore in places, but that was to be expected with the level of enthusiasm in her and Jaq's bedroom antics. Her headache eased, releasing the tension in her shoulders, as the water warmed and heated her body. The only thing out of place was the fatigue and lack of energy she felt. Like she'd been overloaded and her body was shielding itself while it recovered.

Her energy was still there she realized, but something had triggered a defense mechanism within her, temporarily cutting off access to the strongest of her energy. Enora's phone began to buzz in the other room. She knew it would have something to do with whatever happened last night, but for now, she let it ring while she gathered her thoughts.

.....

"Alright, everyone is present and accounted for," Disrayan said before taking a seat on Farrah's couch.

They had decided to meet at Farrah's apartment because it was closest to the gate to Ceres. Not that it mattered as the gate was closed again. Jaq had confirmed it on his way to Farrah's apartment.

Disrayan had been the first to arrive, even before Farrah, Donovan, and Zazzie had arrived from the monster house. The three of them were still covered in the dirt from the forest floor from when they passed out. A literal dirt nap.

It lifted the mood a little for Jaq to see his future brother in law so disheveled. The man had a serious stick up his ass, and despite their newfound common ground with the alliance, Jaq still couldn't help seeing the guy knocked down a peg or two.

"Any ideas on what the hell happened?" Zazzie asked, twirling one of her long locks around her finger.

Jaq admired the curve of her ass in the tight jeans she wore but averted his gaze when he felt Farrah's disapproving glare. He may be in love with Enora, but that didn't mean he couldn't appreciate a woman with natural beauty.

"Why don't we each go over our experience of what happened? The more detail the better. That way we can have a better idea," Donovan said.

Enora blushed and refused to look at Jaq. He smirked and shook his head.

"I'll go first. I was balls deep in a black beauty when what I thought was a real fucking intense orgasm turned into an unexpected nap."

Enora's head whipped around, her eyes shooting daggers even as her cheeks flamed red like cherry wood.

"I think we can skip those kinds of details," she snapped.

"Agreed," Farrah said, shooting daggers at Jaq as well.

"Fine, Enora, what were you up to?"

Jaq couldn't help poking at her. He was still a little pissed about her trying to merge their energy earlier. Not that he hadn't thought about merging with her before. He just wanted to be sure she was his and his alone before he let that happen.

She cleared her throat and smoothed her button-down shirt before speaking. "I was reading and thought a migraine was coming on. I woke with my book on my face."

Jaq shook his head at her obvious lie. Yet, he knew the others would buy it. Enora kept this prim and proper act around everyone, including him. At least until, he got her into bed.

"I was already sleeping when it happened, but Mack felt a rush of energy that almost knocked him unconscious. He knew it affected me when he couldn't wake me to see if I had felt it too," Disrayan said.

"Mack didn't pass out? Where is he now?"

"No idea. He made sure I was okay and said he had to check on something," Disrayan said.

Donovan raised an eyebrow at her answer and pulled out his phone. Jaq knew he was calling Mack and got a little worried when his cousin didn't answer Donovan's call either.

Disrayan started to pace the room. Something wasn't sitting right with what was going on. No way Mack would leave Disrayan's side after something like that, unless it was major. On top of that, Disrayan didn't seem all pissed about his lack of presence either, meaning she at least had an idea of what he was doing but wasn't going to say.

Secrets and lies abound. The only people who told the truth about their whereabouts and what they were doing were Farrah, Donovan, and Zazzie.

"Speaking of missing cousins, has anyone heard from Hendrex?"

"He's in Ceres," Zazzie answered.

Of course, she would know where Hendrex was. They weren't so good at hiding their feelings for one another. They were just too stupid to admit it out loud to each other. Something Jaq would be sure to rib Hendrex about when all of this was over.

"Alright, we know it happened late at night and that it was some sort of massive energy surge. The Security Force in Ceres would have picked up on something that large. What doesn't make sense is why they would close the gate again and not send people to investigate," Jaq said.

"Well, aren't you the expert?" Farrah laughed.

"When you are on the watch list, you learn a few things," he said.

"You are not on a watch list," Donovan sighed.

"Not a watch list, THE watch list. Just because you dropped things because you're with Farrah, doesn't mean your pops doesn't see me as any less of a threat to the status quo," Jaq said.

Enora snorted.

"What status quo? That asshole Ruling Three destroyed it when he had Hendrex removed as Ruling Four."

"Speaking of Ruling Three. I found out some information while they were sentencing Hendrex."

Farrah leaned forward and grabbed one of the many notebooks she had around her house.

"Do tell," she said.

"Ruling Three is definitely up to something. I read something in the Archives about a Ruling Fifth and how he almost rid Ceres of the Council in his quest to be the sole ruler. He was power hungry but

19

also a little mad. They original ruling families figured out his plan in time to stop him and changed the position of Ruling Fifth to the Magistrate," Disrayan said.

Farrah's pen stopped scratching furiously on the pad for her to stare at Disrayan with wide eyes.

"You mean all of this was because that bastard wants to rule Ceres by himself?"

"I don't have proof of anything. I'm just saying he may be taking advantage of the Barrier situation for political gain."

"Or he caused the Barrier situation to create the conditions for him to gain power," Jaq offered.

Enora shook her head. "That doesn't make any sense. Disrupting the Barrier to that extent nearly destroyed Ceres. Why would anyone desperate to rule the place try to destroy it?"

"Look, guys, right now, it's just a theory. We don't have any proof he has done anything more than be an asshole."

Donovan went to the kitchen to grab a glass of water. After chugging it, he set the cup down and cleared his throat.

"I don't like any of this. It's all too convenient not to be connected. We just need to pull the right threads to unravel this mystery before the worst happens."

Jaq moved from his spot on the couch and headed for the door.

"I'm gonna go track down Mack. Y'all let me know if you find anything real to all this talk."

With that, he left, only he wasn't going to find Mack. Not yet anyway. He had a stop to make before he tracked his errant cousin. He'd received texts from members of The Resistance about the surge last night. Everyone, including the few Vampires and Shifters in the group, had felt something. He needed to check in with Tyr.

.....

Tyr was wearing a track in the dirt with all of his pacing. His pack had been hit hard by whatever the energy surge had been last night. Many still had yet to recover. Youngsters on the verge of their first shift had all changed simultaneously, and some hadn't found their way home yet.

"Babe, it's going to be okay."

Sequoia placed a hand on his arm, forcing him to halt. He looked into her eyes; concern clear on her face.

"As much as I want a family, I'm grateful we haven't had pups yet," he said, and she frowned.

"We have Sarah."

"I know we have Sarah. I'm just saying. I don't think I could have handled what happened last night knowing we had a baby or one on the way. There is no telling what a surge like that could have done."

"Sheila says her pups are fine. A little cranky and tired but otherwise, nothing out of the ordinary. The midwife is already checking on Ruby. We'll know soon if it affected her baby. Aside from a few errant teens and the groups on watch in the city, everyone is accounted for."

"Have you heard from Raya?"

Sequoia nodded. "She didn't feel anything back home. She is, however, on her way to make sure we're okay."

Tyr snorted.

"That's the last thing I need right now, a non-pack nosy as fuck bird Shifter," he grumbled.

Sequoia gripped his arm tighter, her nails digging into his biceps.

"Watch your temper, love."

"I could say the same to you."

Tyr took her mouth with his, and the tension eased from his body as he got lost in his mate. He pulled away and sighed; her much needed distraction technique had worked. He was able to focus on what needed to get done now that he wasn't overanalyzing everything. Starting with making sure everyone in his pack was in the loop about the new threat. Word would have traveled fast among his active spies, but that still left one wolf out of the equation. Reign was borderline rogue at this point. The lack of finding a mate at his age was taking its toll. Especially considering he was too uptight to relieve his physical needs with anyone less.

"I need to check on Reign. He left for some time in seclusion, but this mess warrants breaking the rules on that."

Sequoia smiled.

"That's my Alpha. Now that you are acting yourself, I can tell you. You have a visitor."

Tyr frowned.

"Visitor?"

He didn't have to wonder long; a stiff breeze blew a familiar scent in his direction.

"If I didn't already know you were friends, I'd be a little worried about the leader of The Resistance showing up unannounced," Sequoia laughed and walked away before he could reply.

He had never mentioned his connection with Jaq Andromeda to Sequoia, but as his mate, she was privy to things about him that most others weren't.

"To what do I owe the pleasure of this visit?" Tyr tried to play it cool, but Jaq was too keen to fall for it.

"I see your pack was hit last night too," he said.

Tyr sighed and signaled Jaq to follow him away from anyone that may overhear their conversation.

"Do you know what happened?"

"I came here to ask you the same thing. Aura around Langsmith all passed out and have experienced issues with their abilities since the surge."

"Is that what you're calling it? The surge?"

"Yeah, after piecing together a few people's stories and the timeline, it seems there was some sort of ripple effect. Those closest to the city were hit the hardest. Some haven't even woken yet."

"Shit," Tyr cursed.

"Yeah, tell me about it. I was in the middle of a good thing when my ass got knocked out. Talk about embarrassing," Jaq said.

Tyr couldn't help but laugh. Jaq was a what some would call a womanizer. He and Tyr had torn through the singles scene together before Tyr found Sequoia. Now Jaq's exploits only highlighted for Tyr how lucky he was to have a biological switch that recognized when he met his mate. Tyr didn't know that much about Aura mating practices, but he knew it was fraught with as much uncertainty as their human cousins. He may have outgrown his wild youth but that didn't mean Tyr was going to let that gem of a confession go without response.

"Aww, your human not take to kindly about you conking out before she got hers?"

"Oh, she got hers, multiple times. Anyway, that isn't the point. I know you have people on watch around the city. I know you can't tell me specifics, but they could help us track where the surge originated from. Most Aura live on the same side of town, so there's no telling from them."

Tyr sobered at the reminder of just how serious this was.

"We are pretty far outside of town, and it hit us pretty hard. I haven't heard from half my crews in the downtown and warehouse districts," he said.

"Well, that's a place to start."

"I can't leave the pack right now. Things are still too unsettled. Would you mind having your Resistance buddies tour those two areas and report back on any unusual nappers or animals in the area?"

Jaq smirked.

"Sure thing, bro. I'm glad you're okay."

"I'm sorry your night was ruined."

"Man, mated life has really got you in touch with your feelings," Jaq laughed.

Tyr flicked him off and shot him a glare.

"Don't be mad your mate hasn't accepted you yet. Enora is a sweet girl, by the way."

Tyr enjoyed the moment of Jaq's surprise, but just as soon as the shock flashed in his eyes, it was gone, replaced by the cool exterior Jaq reserved for those he didn't know so well.

"Keep your Shifter snout out of my personal business," Jaq snapped.

Tyr ignored the edge in the other man's voice. Any sane man would get defensive about their mate, especially when they were keeping it a secret for whatever reason.

"Just know that a woman like Enora won't appreciate such crass talk about your interactions. If you want her to take you seriously, toning that down will go a long way."

"Whatever, man. I'll check out downtown, and you straighten shit up here. I'll let the rest of the X-men know you're good."

"Not the X-men," Tyr laughed, watching his friend sulk away.

Teasing Jaq about his relationship with the medical examiner had been a fun distraction, but now that Jaq was gone, Tyr had to put his Alpha face back on and make sure his pack was okay.

.....

The ground shook beneath Hendrex's feet, the thick greige fog that hung over Magelor since the Barrier Incident had now reached the ground, like the walls of Ceres were closing in with every tremor. Hendrex didn't know what happened last night to cause such a drastic shift in the Barrier's stability, but whatever it was, he needed to get his people out before Ceres collapsed. Well, not his people anymore. They had chosen to remove him from his leadership position. The verdict still stung, but while his ego was bruised, Hendrex couldn't sit idle when the people he cared for were in danger.

Hendrex stewarded a few scared families to the Garden Gate only to find it sealed. He rubbed his chest, a slow ache spreading there as his muscles contracted and tensed with fear and the fight to draw air into his lungs instead of the dirty simulated clouds that now choked the city streets. It was his worst nightmare realized. The people of Ceres were panicked. Residents who had suffered from the Barrier Incident passed him with solemn and accusatory glares, as if he had something to do with this.

The Meeting House was surrounded by a crowd of Aura, chanting, combining their energy to stabilize the Barrier in the same way they had during the Barrier Incident. Hendrex wasn't ready for this déjà vu. His chest tightened more, and his eyes burned with tears. His people, his home, was on the verge of collapse, and he was no longer in a position to do anything about it. He was no longer part of the Ruling Council and, since the trial, an outcast to most of the Aura. Still, he wasn't ready to give up on Ceres, nor his people.

Hendrex pushed into the crowd and joined the chanting. His energy swelled once connected with the others, easing some of the tension inside of him, but when he felt just how unstable the Barrier crystal had become, the tears he held back, slid free. This was it. This would be the end if he didn't do something more. He kept chanting as he moved through the crowd and into the Meeting House.

Commander Mars stood in the middle of the room barking orders at frantic Security Force Officers. For the first time, Hendrex saw the error in keeping the newest and least experienced closest to the seat of power in Ceres. They looked like reckless frightened children as they attempted to follow the Commander's orders.

"We need to open the gate," Hendrex said.

It wasn't a sudden realization, but it felt like one. His words went unnoticed. With a sigh, he marched right up to Commander Mars and placed his hands on the man's shoulders.

"We need to open the gate and evacuate as many as possible!"

This time, the Commander frowned at him.

"The gate shouldn't be closed. I ordered men there hours ago to help people cross."

Hendrex sighed and stepped back. This was not good news at all.

"There was no one at the gate when I brought several families there, and it's sealed. Either we are in bigger trouble than we care to admit, or someone sealed it in the chaos."

Hendrex and the Commander exchanged knowing looks before they bounded up the stairs to the control room. Sure enough, Ruling One and Ruling Three were there channeling their power to the Balancing Crystal, and keeping the gate closed in the process.

Hendrex moved into the room and joined the chanting. He could better help stabilize the Barrier from here anyway. The issue with the gate would have to wait. The last thing he wanted was to start an argument that would lead to the fall of Ceres while there were still innocents in harm's way.

As soon as the Barrier was stable enough, he felt Ruling One begin to recede her energy from the crystal and he did so as well. Ruling Three held on a little longer before pulling back as well.

"We need to open the gate," Hendrex sighed.

Ruling One wiped her brow with a handkerchief she had pulled from the pocket of her robe.

"We just got the Barrier stable again. It wouldn't be wise to reopen the gate and risk undoing all we have done today," she said.

"For once I agree with you," Ruling Three said.

"The Barrier is never going to be stable. It hasn't been stable since the incident and it is getting worse. We need to evacuate and save what we can while we still can," Hendrex argued.

Both Ruling Three and Ruling One eyed him suspiciously.

"Who let you up here in the first place? You have no right to be here," Ruling Three said.

Commander Mars stepped forward and held up his hand.

"I escorted Hendrex here. With the Council suspended, I am in charge, and I agree with him. The gate must be opened. Not only to give the people a choice in if they stay in this turmoil, but to not further isolate those outside of the Barrier. We are all still Aura, and until the elections happen, I demand the gate be reopened."

Ruling One looked taken aback while Ruling Three scowled. Both looked ready to protest, but a small crowd of young Security Force Officers had gathered. Hendrex had a feeling Ruling Three did as the Commander asked because there was no way he could justify doing otherwise without looking like the ass Hendrex and Commander Mars knew him to be. Ruling One waved them both off and left the room. Depleted after holding the Barrier energy for so long, she wouldn't have been of much help anyway.

Ruling Three and Hendrex exchanged glances before tapping back into the Barrier's energy source and opening the gate. Once again, Ruling Three waited until Hendrex withdrew his energy before withdrawing his own.

"I don't like this situation one bit. I demand that elections be moved up posthaste. We are not a military establishment. We need the expertise of a seasoned Council to deal with this issue," Ruling Three said before sweeping out of the room.

Commander Mars shook his head and signaled for Hendrex to get going. Hendrex knew it wasn't personal. There was just so much to do and to deal with now that the Barrier was stable and the gate was reopened. Hendrex's first duty was to ensure he got as many people out of Ceres as he could before anything else went wrong. Then, he would check in with his friends on the outside and see what new developments had transpired.

Trouble

Three wolves rounded the corner as Jaq drove into the warehouse district. They took one look at him and headed in the opposite direction. With a curse, Jaq hopped out of the car and took off after them. They were slow enough that Jaq was able to raise a wall of energy to block their path.

That was the first sign that they were affected by the surge. The second was that as soon as Jaq was in biting range, they all shifted back to human form, lethargic and out of breath.

"Help us," the lead wolf said before he collapsed on the ground.

"Shit," Jaq cursed.

He looked around to see if anyone else had seen three wolves turn into naked men before passing out. The area was empty, and Jaq caught the Shifters close enough to his car that he could help them one by one. If he could keep them awake long enough. Jaq gave a quick energy zap to one of the men who woke with a gasp.

"Come on, man, can you at least get to your feet?"

The man's eyes turned golden, and the sound of cracking bone echoed against the warehouse walls.

"Run," the man uttered before the shift overcame him.

Jaq jumped back in time to miss the first snap of the wolf's jaws, but not the second. It tore into the sleeve of his coat as the wolf fell to the ground. His heart raced in his chest as he stared at the unconscious wolf. He was going to need back up.

Dealing with friendly Shifters was one thing, but the man was too weak to control his wolf's base instinct. The Aura and Shifters weren't natural enemies, but there was something to be said for generational knowledge. The war against magic users had far reaching effects that despite the more civilized world still had a hold on some. It was one of the things The Resistance worked to improve.

Reaching into his pocket, Jaq found his phone and dialed Tyr. If anyone was going to get these wolves back into Shifter territory, it would be other Shifters. Once Tyr was notified, Jaq called Jasmine, his second in command, and instructed her to inform the others about disoriented Shifters running around the city. Everyone needed to be on alert to avoid war starting offenses. The surge was bad enough without these troublesome consequences.

Jaq pushed the unconscious wolf back toward the others and used his energy to keep them unconscious until help could arrive. It was the safest way for everyone, but it left Jaq feeling more drained than usual. The surge had done a real number on him, even if he hadn't been able to admit that to Enora earlier.

A noise from the other end of the alley caught his attention. He hoped it was Tyr's men, but a Vampire stumbled along near the alley. Jaq held his breath as he concentrated on bending the light energy around himself and the fallen Shifters. The last thing he needed was a Vampire picking a fight, or worse, looking for a snack when Jaq was already compromised.

Sweat dripped from his brow and a dull ache began to form in the middle of his brow. The Vampire stood at the entrance of the alley, barely able to stay on his own two feet. His body swayed with the breeze as his heightened senses picked up on things his eyes couldn't see. After a tense moment, the Vampire kept moving, ambling away on the search for its next meal. Jaq held the shield a little longer to be on the safe side, and when he released it, he too needed to sit for a bit. His body ached, and a cold sweat broke out all over his skin. He felt like his stomach was going to betray him at any moment, but his exhaustion turned to overwhelming relief when a larger than normal hawk flew overhead, diving just low enough to check out the scene before it let out a screech. A few minutes later, three men came ambling into the alley carrying duffel bags, which Jaq could only assume held clothes for the three naked Shifters beside him.

"You should see a healer," one of the Shifters said as he helped one of his pack to his feet.

Jaq nodded before forcing himself to stand.

"That's my next stop. I have my people on the lookout for more of your buddies," Jaq said and headed back to his car.

He was overworked and exhausted, but only one healer came to mind. It wasn't the brightest idea to bother Enora at work, but he was overcome with a need to see her. To make sure she was safe and well. The full effects of the surge were worse than he thought, and Enora had already shown signs of being more effected than he was this morning. Mind made up, Jaq headed straight there.

.....

"The gate's open," Disrayan said and grabbed her purse.

Enora sighed and got up. Now that the gate was open, she had no reason to continue to shirk her responsibilities.

"You guys keep me informed. I'm going to head into work. See if this incident caused any casualties. Human or otherwise."

"That's a good idea," Farrah said and gave her a hug before walking her to the door.

Enora got to work later than she expected. The streets had been packed with people, out and about for the brief period of nice weather in the afternoon. If she didn't know any better, Enora would assume that nothing strange had occurred last night. Yet the weakness she still felt in her limbs was a reminder that it had in fact happened.

"Good Afternoon, Doctor Circinus."

Enora smiled at the young man who worked behind the receptionist counter. He was chubby and loved reading comic books during his downtime. He'd had a rough introduction to Donovan and Farrah earlier that year, but since then his people skills had improved.

29

Once in her small office, Enora slid on her lab coat and checked the logs from the overnight shift. Nothing out of the ordinary was reported although there was a note about an influx of unconscious patients at the hospital that could mean a rush of bodies later.

Enora hoped that wasn't true. After last night, she wasn't sure she'd be up to guiding more spirits into the afterlife. Especially confused ones who had no idea how or even why they'd died. Working with death wasn't a glamorous job, by any means. It was messy, and the smell could stick to you at times depending on what stage of decomposition the body was in when it arrived.

She went into the cold room to pull out one of the corpses labeled for autopsy. It was a young boy who had been identified as a missing teen a few weeks before. His family had already IDed the body and just wanted answers as to how their son died.

After a thorough examination, Enora sighed and shook her head. There were no visible bite marks on the boy, but she knew a transition gone wrong when she saw one. His skin was waxy and pale, and his gum line was red and swollen in the canine region. Eyes bloodshot, and blood mixed with alcohol was found in his stomach without any trace of internal injury.

As many women who had gone missing in the city, young boys were turning up dead with equal frequency. The Vampires needed to get a handle on their rogue situation. Enora could only cover for them so much, and frankly, she was tired of it. Especially knowing that the blood in this boy's stomach had been laced with Aura blood. Blood stolen from her own people. It was maddening and frustrating. She didn't envy the people who had to explain what she wrote as the cause of death to the parents of these kids.

She just wished she could do more, but her talents were best-suited for behind the scenes work, not the front lines. She would leave that to Farrah and Donovan. No, better yet, to Zazzie who worked in the schools and often acted as the first line of defense to keep these kids on the straight and narrow. So much for not being depressed at work today. Enora could compartmentalize with the best of them, but the surge had knocked out all of her coping mechanisms.

With a sigh, she went back to her office to tackle the mountain of paperwork that always seemed to be waiting. She preferred the more hands on part of her job, but today, she couldn't stomach it. She was just getting into the groove of things when there was a knock on her door. She frowned when she saw Jaq standing in the doorway.

"You shouldn't be here," she snapped, and he shrugged.

"I wanted to finish what was interrupted last night," he said.

Enora rolled her eyes and pointed to the exit.

"One, I am at work. Two, you are not allowed back here without signing in and having the proper credentials. Three, you have lost your mind if you think I would ever do anything like that here."

Jaq smirked and moved closer to her desk, leaning across the surface until his face was mere inches from hers.

"Live a little, will ya?" he said before brushing his lips across hers.

She couldn't help the warmth that spread through her body with even the smallest of interactions with Jaq. He was her kryptonite, but she couldn't get distracted by him. Not here, and not now.

"Jaq," Enora hated how breathy and pleading she sounded as she said his name, "Get out."

Jaq sighed and pulled away, but the sound of feet stomping down the hall made them both pause. Before Enora could say anything, Jaq had come around her desk and ducked under it in time for Detective Burns to walk through the open door.

"Sorry to bother you, Dr. Circinus, but I need the cause of death for my case."

Enora forced a tight smile and nodded.

"I was just getting to the paperwork for that," she replied, shuffling through the stack of papers to find the notes she had written an hour ago.

Of course, her meticulous organization had been ruined when Jaq had interrupted, and she hadn't realized how shuffled things had gotten as they kissed. Frustrated with herself for taking so long, she forgot Jaq was hiding under her desk until she felt him unzip her work pants. She shuffled papers frantically to cover the rasping noise as his hand slid into the opening to cup her sex.

"It was right here, sorry, I'm just out of it today," she explained as she tried to focus on the task at hand, instead of Jaq's hand as he

31

pressed two fingers inside of her.

She bit her lip to keep from moaning as they dipped and swirled inside her; the friction of his palm rubbing on her clit already pushing her to the edge of release.

Burns frowned at her.

"You don't seem well. Is everything okay?" he asked.

"Yes!" Enora cringed at her overenthusiastic exclamation that had more to do with Jaq and less to do with answering the detective's question.

"Sorry, I mean, last night was long, and I'm a little exhausted but fine," she rambled.

Burns nodded.

"Yeah, last night was a rough one for us at the precinct. Reports of wild animal sightings in downtown, coupled with people having a mass black out. That's why I want to wrap this case up. I have at least ten new ones on my desk right now," he said.

"Ahhh, yes," she hissed as Jaq tugged her pants lower to get better access. "That does sound... intense."

She shifted in her chair to facilitate Jaq's actions. In doing so, a stack of papers shifted and she found the notes she was looking for.

"There they are," she said and handed the paperwork to Detective Burns. "You can make a photocopy down the hall and return them to me later. I don't want to keep you from your work."

That wasn't protocol, and not anything she would ever do, but Detective Burns didn't look like he was going to argue, even as he gave her a quizzical look.

"Okay, I'll just be out of your hair then. I'll get this back to you ASAP." Detective Burns turned to leave.

"Oh, can you close the door on your way out? I need to concentrate to get back on top of things," Enora said.

Detective Burns gave her the once over, his eyes briefly fixating at the small gap between the bottom of her desk and the floor and shook his head.

"Sure thing, Doc," he said, giving her a wink before closing the door.

Enora didn't have time to ponder the embarrassment of being caught in such a compromising position. As soon as the door was closed, Jaq pulled her pants the rest of the way down and pulled her hips forward. She nearly fell out of the chair as he tossed her legs over his shoulders before his mouth descended upon her core.

"I thought he'd never leave," Jaq grumbled against her.

His thick lips and hot tongue slid along her exposed flesh, his fingers thrusting to punctuate every word. Her body clenched and shivered around him, her hips moving of their own volition, grinding against his face and hands, demanding every ounce of pleasure he had to offer.

"Fuck you, Jaq," she breathed, enjoying every minute of her orgasm and hating herself for being so weak for him.

The idea of him tongue fucking her in her place of work should only be hot in theory, a fantasy to be played out in the bedroom. Not in reality, and not when she knew she'd already been caught. Yet, here she was, dripping wet and ready for more. Decorum, professionalism, and hygiene be damned.

"Love, I hope you do," he chuckled sliding up her body, his own pants already undone.

He took her mouth with his, the musky tang of her climax coating his tongue and lips added to the rush of danger Enora felt in the moment. She clenched her thighs around his waist.

"Don't call me love," she said, and he smirked.

"Why not? Love," he said before tearing open the condom he'd produced from his jeans pocket with his teeth.

"I don't want false endearments. Save those for your other women," Enora sighed, unable to look him in the eye.

Part of their agreement was Jaq was not allowed to discuss his other women with her. She wasn't naïve enough to think Jaq would ever be a one-woman man. She had never even asked that he try. Knowing he had others was a blatant reminder of why she could never take him seriously. At least, not in the relationship department.

.....

A knife to the heart. That's what Enora's words felt like. *How could she think so low of him? Then again, how could she not?* Their whole relationship was built on casual fucking. She had never demanded

33

monogamy, and to be truthful, he had been with others at first. Habits were hard to break, but he'd done it for her.

Jaq slid the condom on and positioned himself at her core. The tip of his dick was like a heat seeking missile determined to dive in and blow up her spot. Yet, he needed her to know that this wasn't just about sex for him. Not anymore, and to be honest, it never had been.

He leaned forward, barely pressing into her. She gasped and shuddered before grabbing his hips and pulling him closer. She was so wet for him he couldn't control the momentum as he slid home until his hips pressed firm against her pelvis.

Her muscles clenched and released around his cock as if urging him deeper.

"You are my only love," he groaned before the last shred of his control snapped.

He rolled his hips before pulling back and sliding into her once more.

"Jaq." Enora's cry was more a hoarse whisper.

Even in the throes of passion, she still had enough sense to realize she was at work. A detail Jaq himself had almost forgotten as soon as he'd gotten his dick in her. He hadn't been lying about finishing what they had started last night. The problem was seeing Enora so in her element. The buttoned up professional side of Enora gave him serious hot for teacher vibes. It would take great restraint not to embarrass himself like an inexperienced school boy. Jaq had to get a handle on himself quick, nothing was going to make him finish before he could show her just how much he loved and worshiped her.

Jaq closed his eyes and focused on keeping a steady rhythm. Slowing and speeding up to match Enora's thrusting hips and praying he wouldn't make a fool of himself a second time in a row. Her breathing became more erratic, her thrusting more frantic, and her inner muscles put his dick in a vice grip before she exploded. He captured her keening moan with a kiss as his own body shuddered with release. She clung tight to him as they rode out the waves of pleasure.

"I mean it, Enora. You are the only woman for me, my love."

She stiffened in his arms before pulling away. The warm glow of her post-orgasmic bliss faded in an instant. She moved away from him as if he had burned her and began to redress.

"You need to get out of here. I can't believe I just let you do this." She was flustered and once again, shutting him out. Pushing him away as soon as he broached the topic of them being anything more than fuck buddies.

With a sigh, he pulled off the used condom and tossed it in the red can marked biohazard in the corner before pulling up his own pants.

"Well, let me know when you're ready to let me do it again," Jaq huffed before storming out of her office.

He'd been an idiot to come to her place of work. He'd meant to ask her on a date and ended up proving to her once again that he was good for nothing but casual sex. He'd have to keep better check on his libido the next time he had a chance. If she gave him another chance after he so expertly confessed his love in the middle of impromptu office sex.

Caught up in his thoughts, Jaq ran straight into Detective Burns. The man was returning the paperwork Enora had let him use.

"Sorry, man." Jaq tried to make their interaction short, but Detective Burns grabbed his arm.

"It's really not my place, but I've known Dr. Circinus for a few years now. I'm glad she has found someone, but know if you hurt her, you won't be able to so much as jaywalk without someone from the precinct on your ass," he said.

Jaq smirked.

"You're right, it's not your place." Jaq removed the man's hand from his arm, giving the man a gentle shock with his energy. Strong enough for the man to notice but nothing more than a strong static shock could produce.

The man shook out his hand, still scowling as Jaq walked away.

. . . . .

Mack tapped the steering wheel of his car with his thumb and alternated glancing between his side view and rearview mirrors. The roads were clear, but Mack couldn't help but be paranoid. Last night, there had been a massive energy surge, one that he had only been close to experiencing once in his lifetime. Molly hadn't been at her condo, and there was only one other place she could be. He just hoped he found her there, and she was safe. That Shane and everyone were safe. Molly's energy had knocked out every other Aura in the city.

Whatever caused her to lose it like that couldn't be anything good. The guard at the gate of the Maura's Men mansion waved him inside with a smile. At least, the man didn't seem on edge. Maybe Mack was being paranoid. He could have called, but cell reception wasn't much better after the surge either.

Greg, a newly transitioned Vampire, sat alone on the front steps. He looked up as Mack approached, a tense set to his shoulders. Mack didn't know Greg very well. Only that he was the brother of Claude's mate Gretchen, and he was ex-military.

"Hey, man. Now is not exactly a good time," Greg said when Mack approached.

"Why not?"

"The happy couples are indisposed. Why do you think I'm out here in the cold?" he said.

"Maybe you were enjoying some fresh air after being holed up in the mansion for the last few months?"

Greg shook his head.

"I've gotten better with controlling my heightened senses, but it's a little hard to shut out three mated couples fucking like they have a new lease on life. Especially, when one member of said couples is your baby sister."

Mack grimaced.

"Right, well. I can offer you a ride into town."

Greg contemplated it for but a moment before getting into the passenger side of Mack's car.

"I almost died last night. Why not?" he said.

"Died?"

Mack turned over the engine on his car and drove back down the long gravel drive.

"Yeah, after that fiasco of a dinner, I took Carrie back to her place. She was pretty upset, understandably, so I stayed behind to make sure she didn't do anything stupid."

"Did she?"

"Of course, she took off by herself, and there was someone following her. It turned out it was one of Maura's Men."

Mack shook his head.

"Maura? I thought she was dead." Mack feigned innocence on that front.

"The bitch is now; Molly took care of her. Anyway, I thought you knew she was the one who turned me."

"I don't know everything," Mack said with a shake of his head.

"Right, sorry. All of this is super new to me. I thought you were in the loop," Greg said.

"Only when I need to be," Mack replied.

They rode the rest of the way making casual small talk. Greg was much chattier than Mack had anticipated, but then again, the man had spent months locked away at the Maura's Men mansion while he adjusted to the transition of being a Vampire, and one of Maura's Men at that. It still struck Mack that he had been so blind to the fact that Greg was also one of Maura's Men. His energy didn't read as dark as the others. It was torture for Mack not to ask more details about Greg's turning.

They were pulling into downtown when Mack caught some suspicious movements out of the corner of his eye. He wasn't the only one who noticed either. Greg, though nonchalant the whole ride, had kept his head on the swivel the entire time. Mack could appreciate a man who could be sociable and alert at the same time. Mack parked his car a few blocks from Club Obelisk.

As he stepped from his car, a Vampire ran up on him, slamming him against the hood. In an instant, Greg was there tossing the Vampire off of Mack. It was broad daylight in the middle of downtown, and the two were brawling like they were in a private gym. Mack didn't have time to step in to help because almost as soon as the fight got started it was over. Greg had the Vampire pinned to the ground.

"Maximus wants his daughter back," the Vampire hissed.

"Who?" Mack and Greg said in unison.

The Vampire on the ground had the nerve to laugh.

"I see Carrie hasn't been honest with her new friends. Did you think you could run off with a royal blood Vampire and get away with it?"

Mack frowned as Greg punched the Vampire one good time in the mouth.

"If she wanted to run home to Daddy, she would. Tell Maximus he can piss off."

Greg let the Vampire go, and he took off, leaving Mack to stare incredulously at Greg.

"Okay, I need to be in the loop right now."

Greg ran a hand down his face and shrugged.

"Sure, just someplace less out in the open. I don't want to be caught off-guard again."

Mack nodded and led Greg to the Club. It would be closed this time of day, but Mack had a key. Once seated at the bar, Mack poured Greg a shot of bourbon and leaned against the counter.

"Alright, what the hell am I missing?"

Greg sighed and downed the shot before signaling Mack to pour another.

"You want the long version or the short version?"

Mack pulled out another glass and took a shot of bourbon with Greg.

"Long, I need all the details if my life is apparently in danger over this."

Greg nodded.

"I'm not sure of everything myself. I just know that Maura wanted Carrie to get revenge on Shane. I almost died again trying to protect her. She's fine, by the way, sleeping last night off at the mansion. At least, for today. I'm pretty sure she'll be hightailing it out of here once she is rested enough. Molly made it pretty clear that Carrie is not welcome, and after seeing Molly go head to head with Maura last night, I don't blame her for wanting to get out of dodge when she is on Molly's bad side."

Mack filled in the gaps where he could, but none of it made any sense.

"Carrie was at the rehab center with Shane. Do you think she is some sort of Vampire psycho? Born Vampires are rare; female born

Vamps are even more rare. She should be locked in some gilded tower with a private physician, not gallivanting with drug addicts in a rehab facility. Maybe we need to return her to Maximus before anyone else gets hurt."

"I've met my fair share of psychos. Carrie isn't one of them. A little quirky and sheltered but not a psycho."

Mack caught the small smile that threatened to break through as Greg spoke about Carrie, and he had to wonder if something else had gone on between them last night.

"Don't look at me like that. I barely know the woman, but she saw how injured I was last night and gave me her blood to heal me quicker. If that doesn't speak to her character, then I don't know what does."

The shot glass Mack held nearly slipped from his fingers.

"She gave you her blood? Like from a glass or?"

Greg frowned and poured his own shot before downing it.

"From the source."

Mack coughed a few times and put the bottle of bourbon away before they both drank away his next paycheck.

"Hmm, well, either way. It's not a good idea for any of us to get in the way of Maximus and his daughter. As for what happened last night, whatever Molly did to get rid of Maura had some far reaching effects that might make this town a bit of a powder keg."

"Well, I know Maximus won't be coming at us with any force for a while. His A-team got destroyed in the fighting last night," Greg snorted.

Mack rolled his eyes.

"Let me help you understand something. For one, there are more Vampires than just Maximus who will come after Carrie now that word is out that she is here. Second, there are more supernaturals in Langsmith than just Vampires. Last night hit the supernatural community hard, and someone is going to be the fall guy. When fingers start wagging, I'd rather not be at the center of a supernatural war."

Greg rose an eyebrow at Mack.

"What kind of other supernaturals?"

The question went unanswered as Mack's phone buzzed in his pocket. He pulled it out and sighed when he saw it was a text from

39

Jaq calling an emergency meeting of the X-men ASAP. He had already missed the meeting at Farrah's earlier, so he couldn't bow out of this one without raising suspicions, yet he wasn't done talking with Greg. Mack wasn't sure it was a good idea to bring Greg in on everything, but his military experience could be an asset, and with the rest of Maura's Men indisposed, they were short a Vampire delegate for the meeting.

"Come with me, and you'll find out."

Secrets and Lies

Ruling Three reveled in the surge of energy from the onlookers as he moved behind the podium at the center of the refugee camp. He'd set up this meeting as soon as Commander Mars made it clear what side he was on. Winning over the people without the support of the Security Force Commander was unheard of. The Commander was well-respected and known for being apolitical. If Ruling Three had any shot of making his dream a reality, he needed to act fast to rid himself of all possible obstacles.

There was nothing like the feeling of hundreds of pairs of eyes looking to you with hope and admiration. It was the best part of his job as Ruling Three, having people recognize the power and importance and respecting it. It was a feeling he never wanted to give up, even if that meant destabilizing his people and their home to make it so.

"Ruling Three, what do you think about Ruling Four's evacuation plan?"

The question cut into Ruling Three's reverie, and he frowned.

"Hendrex Andromeda has already proven himself unworthy in the eyes of the people. His faux concern and lack of faith in the power of the Aura is troubling, to say the least. There is no reason for us to leave our home, our sanctuary from the evils of the human world," Ruling Three paused for dramatic effect sweeping his gaze across the murmuring crowd, "If anything, we should rally together as you all have, show that our strength and might has not diminished with time. Stand strong against those who wish to destroy us and our legacy."

He raised his arms, and the crowd cheered. A smile lit his face as he let their adoration sink in. They were eating out of the palm of his hand. Hendrex's actions, while annoying, were helping his cause. Like the human children's book, Hendrex was running around screaming 'the sky is falling' while in reality, it had lowered for a brief time. Ruling Three would set things back to rights as soon as he had complete and sole control of Ceres and the Aura. In the meantime, he had to play his cards right and ensure there was nothing left standing in his way.

"His antics only prove that we need to establish a different criterion for our leadership. No more nepotism. The Andromeda family has proved to be nothing more than troublemakers intent on endangering the secrecy of Ceres and the Aura population as a whole."

Murmurs of agreement ran through the crowd.

"While Commander Mars and his family have served valiantly throughout the history of Ceres, it is clear they are in league with the Andromedas. Set on expanding their families' control of Ceres through the binding of Donovan Mars and Farrah Andromeda. Even the position of Magistrate has fallen to the Andromedas' corruption. Magistrate Disrayan has also proven herself in league with the Andromedas through her friendship with Farrah, her relationship with Maclovis, and through her defense of Hendrex Andromeda, despite his clear incompetency."

"What about the Barrier?" a voice shouted from the crowd, interrupting his carefully written speech.

Of course, Ruling Three, ever the politician, was ready for any and all questions thrown his way.

"More evidence of the incompetency of the Security Force under Commander Mars. It's his job to ensure the proper coverage on the Balancing Crystal, and his poor management has led to the loss of land and homes within Ceres. Something I plan to remedy as soon as I am back in my rightful place as leader of Ceres."

Ruling Three paused to see if anyone caught his omission of the Council in his declaration, but no one did, or at least, no one spoke out. He smiled at the people and a cheer came from a little boy perched on his father's shoulders in the back of the crowd.

"Re-elect Ruling Three!"

A chuckle rose from the crowd before they joined in with the boy's rallying cry.

"Re-elect Ruling Three! Re-elect Ruling Three!"

He let the cheer continue for a moment longer before he raised his hands and lowered them in a quieting gesture. The smiling crowd responded to his direction.

"Thank you for your vote of confidence. I just wish that I alone had the ability to speed up this dreadful election process. Why do we need weeks of campaigning when you, the people, know what is in your hearts already? You are tired of the status quo, you want change, and it's a shame that you are being denied your right to vote within a shortened time period. Change is needed now, and I'm afraid the powers that be are afraid of that change."

"What can we do about it?" a man in the crowd shouted.

Ruling Three shook his head before smiling.

"Demand a sooner vote. Just as I had the courage to challenge the Andromeda Regime, you the people have the right to demand a sooner election."

It wasn't as subtle of a hint as Ruling Three had planned for his speech, but the crowd was just as receptive to his more brash declaration of action. The crowd started chanting again.

"Action now! Action now!"

All it took was for one person to start moving toward the Meeting House for the whole crowd to move. Soon, Ruling Three was left standing alone at the podium as the crowd took charge of their own destiny. He smiled to himself and smoothed the fabric of his robes before trailing after the crowd. He wanted to see the look on Commander Mars' face when the crowd demanded a sooner election when there was only one viable candidate.

"Re-Elect Ruling Three," he chanted to himself.

Hendrex stood in the shadows watching as Ruling Three tore apart his family and friends. If he didn't already have a reason to hate the man, he surely did so now. The man had strong delusions of grandeur that would be the death of Ceres if the Aura under his thrall didn't wake the fuck up and smell the corruption. With a shake of his head, Hendrex moved back to the established meeting point for families willing to evacuate. There were two more families waiting to be escorted through the Garden Gate.

At least, that gave him a reason to hope. There were still families in Ceres that saw the writing on the wall and weren't willing to risk their family for the pride of being one of the remaining families in Ceres. He smiled at a little girl who clutched her handsewn doll to her chest, her brown eyes full of fear and a little excitement.

"Is this your first trip outside of Ceres?" Hendrex asked, although he already knew the answer.

At her age, it was her first time, and Hendrex wished it would be an easy trip for her, but it wasn't going to be. Traveling between Ceres and Langsmith was rough on the body, even more so now with the Barrier in such a weakened state. The last family had barely made it through conscious. Even Hendrex needed rest between trips.

The little girl nodded, and he cupped her cheek.

"Just hold on tight to your doll and close your eyes. I will carry you through myself if that's okay with you and your parents."

The little girl nodded and looked to her parents for approval. They hesitated before agreeing. Hendrex picked up the girl and walked them to the gate.

"If you have ever been through the gate before, it's a much harder trip now than ever. Just keep pushing forward, don't stop and don't lag behind. If we stay together and stay moving, we will make it to the other side safe."

Hendrex wished he had more encouraging words for them.

"What do we do once we are through?"

At least, Hendrex had a reassuring answer for that.

"The Magistrate and others will be there to help facilitate your transition to the human world."

"You make it sound so permanent," a woman said.

Hendrex sighed.

"I hope it doesn't have to be, but it's an option we all must be prepared for. Now please, follow me." Hendrex didn't wait for more questions before signaling the Security Force officer in the group to lead the way before he fell in with the little girl's family. Another Security Force officer followed behind.

The little girl clung to Hendrex so tight; he wasn't sure if it was the force of travel or the child's death grip that left the welts along his neck when he pushed through to the other side. It wasn't until he was through that he realized the girl was slack in his arms. He rushed her to where Enora led the medical assistance, and she woke the girl with a wave of a smelling salts stick.

Hendrex allowed a medical professional to take the girl from there before he collapsed in an empty chair.

"You are done for the day," Zazzie said walking to him.

The bells around her ankles jingled as she walked, her brightly colored skirt swaying with her hips.

Hendrex sighed and took her hand before pulling her into his lap.

"Not until I keep my promise to you," he said and kissed her.

Zazzie didn't hesitate to return his affection, her tongue teasing the seam of his lips, and he opened for her, eager for the connection. The silver ball of her tongue ring rasped the roof of his mouth. A sensation he would have to get used to but wasn't entirely against. She smelled of cinnamon and spice, and his stomach rumbled at the thought of all the delicious foods associated with that scent.

"Why don't we get you fed and rested first? Fun can come later," she said as she stood, pulling him to his feet with her.

"Yes, please. No 'fun' in the medical area, thanks," Enora snapped, and Zazzie gave her a look before leading Hendrex away.

He knew not to question their friend dynamics but had to wonder what had the otherwise sweet tempered Enora in such a bad mood. Either way, all of his plans would have to wait. As soon as Donovan saw him, Hendrex knew that rest and 'fun' were the last things he would be having that evening.

"Sorry, Zazzie, but I need to steal your man for a few hours,"

Donovan said.

Zazzie put her hands on her hips and shook her head.

"I don't own him, but know that if he comes to harm, I will hex your ass," she said before turning and kissing Hendrex.

"You would really hex someone over me?"

"Damn straight," she laughed before sauntering back toward the medical station to help Enora with the newcomers.

"Who'd have thought Zarovia Monoceros would be so in love with you?"

"Certainly not me," Hendrex said, allowing for a short moment of personal transparency before he put his wall back up. "So, what's wrong now?"

Donovan noted the changed and signaled toward his car.

"Emergency meeting of the minds. I'll explain more on the way."

Hendrex didn't like how cagey Donovan was being, but given the unsure circumstances, he couldn't fault the man.

"By now, you are aware there was a massive surge of energy that knocked out the Aura population outside of Ceres and further destabilized the Barrier," Donovan began as soon as they pulled away from the curb.

"Yes, any leads on that front?"

"I'm getting there. Anyway, it turns out the Aura weren't the only ones affected last night."

"That's understandable. That amount of energy would certainly have further reaching effects. Has anyone tied the surge to the Aura?"

Donovan shook his head.

"No, but there is Vampire involvement. I'd tell you more, but I think it's best if we wait until we meet with the others to get the full picture."

"Others?"

Hendrex didn't like the sound of that. As much as he understood teamwork was necessary in far reaching cases such as this, he didn't like the idea of the Aura and Ceres being so exposed.

"Don't worry, you'll understand why we brought in who we did when you meet them."

Donovan drove to the warehouse district, and once inside one of the buildings, Hendrex couldn't believe his eyes. Tyr Greywulf, the pack leader of the Langsmith Shifters, was laughing and joking with his cousin Jaq, as well as Maclovis and an unknown Vampire. Jaq looked up and smiled mischievously at Hendrex.

"Glad your slow asses could make it. The meeting of the X-men is about to begin."

.....

Enora finished locking the factory and waved the last of the technicians away. It was five in the evening but felt like it was much later. Between the surge last night, Jaq at her office this morning, and then being called out to run medical assistance for families crossing the gate, Enora was done. If only her friends were on the same level.

"So, you going to tell us what is up with you? I mean, I know the surge was rough, but your attitude is shit, and it's centered around male energy," Zazzie asked as soon as they were seated in their usual booth at the local Italian restaurant.

Zazzie's long locks partially covered her face as she leaned forward. If it wasn't for her serious expression, Zazzie would look comical with the multicolored yarn, beads, and bells woven in her hair. Subtle was not a word in her vocabulary. You could always see, hear, and feel her coming from a mile away. She was usually all peace, love, and laughter, but recent events had dimmed even her sparkling personality.

Enora could feel Zazzie's energy poking and prodding at her defenses. The last thing Enora needed was an interrogation on top of everything else. She scowled at her normally peace-making friend and grabbed a menu from the table.

"I thought we agreed no psychic prying in each other's lives," Enora grumbled hiding her face behind the menu.

It would do nothing to block Zazzie's prying, but thankfully, it was enough of a hint that Zazzie sat back and took a sip of her water. The rainbow-colored bangles on her wrists tinkling with her movement. Of the four of them, Zazzie was the most expressive with her nature. The complete opposite of Enora, but somehow that made them closer to each other. For all the shielding Enora carried daily, Zazzie was never really on the receiving end of her cagey behavior, until now.

"True, but you really weren't yourself today, and with everything that's going on, we just want to be sure you're okay," Disrayan offered.

"And we also want to know if we need to be kicking some ass," Farrah chimed in, sliding in next to Disrayan.

She was dressed in all black, except for the brightly colored leather jacket that she tossed over the back of the booth. It was her work uniform. For someone in the detective business, she was certainly not one to blend into a crowd. Even without her bold fashion choices, her height and beauty made her almost impossible to miss.

Now that Farrah had arrived, the real interrogation would likely begin. Farrah was the nosiest of them all. It was no surprise she'd become a private detective after being kicked off the Security Force. She could never just leave things alone. Enora's only hope was that Farrah would be too fixated on whatever case she was working to truly dig into Enora.

"Late as usual," Disrayan chastised.

"I was escorting a family to a safe house," Farrah said.

The two of them were always snipping at each other, despite being the most alike. Both loved to know everything about everyone, but while Disrayan felt the need to control everything and everyone around her, Farrah was more in line with Zazzie's free spirited nature. As kids, it had always been Enora and Disrayan who kept Zazzie and Farrah from being caught in their many dastardly schemes.

"Look, I'm fine, just tired and worried about everything. I'm sorry for being a grouch." Enora hoped they wouldn't dig any further.

"If I hadn't read the sexual energy all over you this afternoon, I would suggest going out and getting laid," Zazzie said.

"That's always your answer to everything, isn't it? Random sex with strangers, fuck all. Male, female, and all in between," Disrayan laughed.

Disrayan's neat bob brushed the collar of her crisp white button down. The robust sound of her laughter was like music to Enora's ears. Disrayan had been through so much lately. Looking at her, you would never imagine she'd recently been kidnapped and almost killed by vampires.

It was good to see her in a better mood, even if it was at their friend's expense. Not that Zazzie would mind. She was unapologetic about her way of life. It was one of the traits Enora envied. No one would think twice about Zazzie having a fling with Jaq.

"Why not? It works and it's fun," Zazzie shrugged.

Farrah laughed.

"Except you're fooling around with Hendrex now, and he is not exactly the fuck all type," she said.

Zazzie shrugged.

"I wouldn't know. The damn surge ruined our night of fun, and I'm sure many others' night as well," Zazzie said wagging her eyebrows at Enora.

Enora's musings were interrupted as she was once again thrown into the hot seat. She tossed the menu and glared at Zazzie. She hoped the heat in her cheeks wasn't visible to her friends as she schooled her face to something more passive.

"I told you I was reading last night," Enora protested.

"Sure, try reading the writing on the wall. Whoever your mystery bae is, you are not okay with the arrangement you have going."

Her words hit a little too close to home for Enora.

"I don't have a bae or mystery bae. Not all of us are jumping on the binding wagon just because Ceres is on the verge of collapse," Enora snapped.

Her friends all stopped what they were doing to stare at her. Enora was the calm one of the group. She didn't lash out with hurtful words. That was Farrah's territory. Enora did her best not to shrink under their intense glares.

So much for keeping it cool, Enora.

"First of all, only Farrah has any binding planned. Second, who says our relationships have anything to do with the mess Ceres is in?" Disrayan said.

Enora rolled her eyes. She may have been out of line to say it out loud, but that didn't mean there wasn't a grain of truth to her words.

"Farrah and Donovan were thrown together because of missing Aura, the first sign that things weren't smooth sailing, and it took the Barrier Incident for them to finally admit they wanted forever with each other. You and Mack are together because the Barrier Incident brought about the trial against Hendrex and you were forced together to get him to testify. Due to the trial and the subsequent removal of Hendrex as Ruling Four, he has finally gotten over some of his martyr attitude to go for what he wants as a man, and that's Zazzie. So, yes, all of your relationships are doom's day fuck alls, and I, for one, am not going to give in to a man who is so completely wrong for me just because the sex is amazing and the world as we know it is ending." Tears streamed down Enora's cheeks as she ranted.

It had been her intention to lay things out in a clinical way, not get so emotional about it. Her out of character behavior was beginning to scare Enora. She pushed her way out of the booth and was halfway to her car before her friends caught up and surrounded her in a giant hug. Being the shortest of the group, her friends literally engulfed her. Too tired to keep fighting it, Enora let her emotional barrier fall for a moment. Allowing her friends' energy to meld with hers in solidarity. The last time they'd done this was when Disrayan lost her parents. They each absorbed a piece of each other's pain, fears, and worries to shoulder the burden together. They'd been friends since childhood, more than that, they had grown to be sisters. It was yet another reminder that Enora wasn't alone, no matter how bad things got. They always had each other.

"Part of me wants to kick your ass for calling the love of my life a doom's day fuck all, but I know you didn't mean it that way." Farrah broke the silence first.

"Oh, I'm still going to kick her ass, but tomorrow, after she finishes crying out her feelings," Disrayan said.

"This is not a soothing huddle, guys, Enora needs relationship help right now," Zazzie added.

"I don't need relationship help. I'm not in a relationship."

"Fine, a situation-ship, which you have every right not to deal with right now. I mean, seriously, the world is ending, after all," Zazzie joked.

"Not funny, Zazzie. This is serious. Tell me who this douche is so we can kick his ass. I'm sure Farrah knows a good spot to hide a body," Disrayan said.

"Actually, that's more Enora's expertise, but seeing as how she would need plausible deniability, I gladly offer body dumping services."

Enora couldn't help but laugh through her tears.

"Honestly, I'm okay. I just have so many emotions right now. I've never been this out of control of my emotions in my life."

"We know, which is why we are so worried," Disrayan said.

Enora pushed out of her friends' grasps to wipe her cheeks.

"Ugh, can we not do this in public? I don't want people to see me like this."

"Sure, we'll head to your place, watch rom coms and yell at how easy those women have it," Zazzie suggested.

Enora wanted to protest, she felt more like being alone, but then again, having her friends over and not for some tragic news or event sounded like a welcome distraction.

"Fine, but no alcohol. We wouldn't want Rye marching down the block to confront Mack's boss again," Enora said.

"Done, and not because I would. His boss is spoken for, but because I have other questions for her that I don't think I want answers to right now."

That peaked Enora's interest.

"Questions like what?" Farrah asked.

"Ugh, we will talk about it later. Let's just have a movie screaming night and relax before the hell starts again tomorrow."

"I'll meet you guys there. We ran out on our food and bill, and I am starving. I'll pay and bring take-out." Zazzie didn't wait for anyone to answer before heading back into the restaurant.

Enora shrugged at Farrah and Disrayan before they linked arms with her and headed toward her place. The sun had set already, and the night air was crisp and refreshing on Enora's overheated cheeks. They walked in companionable silence. One night to chill was all she needed to get back on track, at least, she hoped. If not, then her life was further out of control than she ever imagined it could get.

The group of five was now a group of eight. Tyr couldn't help but feel outnumbered. Three Vampires and four Aura had gathered to discuss some serious issues that occurred over the course of twenty-four hours. Tyr was still trying to wrap his head around everything. Even with the copious amounts of intelligence gathered by Shifters over the years, he couldn't help but feel like this was an unprecedented catastrophe of coincidences.

"So, let's go over this again. Last night, you three fought Maura, Maura's new Vampire army, as well as Vampire Council leader Maximus and Vampire Council forces with the help of an Aura Vampire hybrid?"

"We are still a little fuzzy on the hybrid details, but basically," Claude said.

Mack sighed.

"I suspected Molly may have been a latent Aura before she was turned. I didn't get confirmation until recently, a few nights before Disrayan was attacked. I experienced her energy firsthand and knew for sure," Mack said.

"That doesn't make any sense. If she was Auraless, there is no way to boost her abilities. If anything, her death should have ended any chance of her having energy knowledge," Hendrex interjected.

"We aren't exactly clear on how Molly was turned by Maura. All we know is Dark Magic was involved, and whatever magic or energy, as you say, Maura had was transferred to Molly in the process," Xander said.

"Regardless of how she got her energy knowledge, she has Aura energy and is also a Vampire. Not to mention, her boss battle with Maura resulted in the disruption of the Aura and Shifter communities in the area," Tyr jumped in.

"Not only that, but The Resistance has heard rumors that the surge has somehow bolstered the energy knowledge of people previously thought Auraless. Whatever that surge was, it's powerful and dangerous and causes a whole lot of questions," Jaq said.

"The surge was Molly coming into her energy knowledge, I am sure of it. What I want to know is how are we going to handle the fall out?" Mack said.

Tyr nodded at the man. At least, one of them had some clear vision of what they were facing.

"The Langsmith Shifters, as always, will maintain our distance from this. We are merely observers and record keepers," he said.

Jaq rolled his eyes.

"Is that your entire stance or just the official one?" Jaq laughed.

Smiling, Tyr leaned forward.

"Official stance, but as you know, I have already agreed to help with the matter of the rogue Vampires. If this other issue happens to be part of it, then I will do what I can without jeopardizing my pack's standing in the Shifter community."

The men all nodded in agreement.

"I am no longer a leader in the Aura community, but I pledge my help regardless. None of this situation bodes well for the stability of the Langsmith community," Hendrex said.

It was uncanny how similar Hendrex and Mack were in looks, and yet, so unlike each other in personality. Tyr knew a little of their family history and the feud between the two brothers, but he had never seen them both in one place before. It put his wolf on edge to be in the presence of such powerful unknowns. Not to mention, Tyr wasn't so pleased with the addition of two unknowns at such an important meeting. He had no prior dealings with Hendrex to have reason to trust the man other than the word of his friends, plus there was the other unknown, a Vampire, who sat quietly observing them all. Even Xander and Claude seemed shocked at Greg's inclusion in the meeting. Tyr didn't know the other two Vampires well, but if they weren't happy about his inclusion then neither was he.

"As always, we will be of service when you need us. With Maura out of the way, we can help with tracking the rogue Vampires who are targeting the Aura and Shifters in the area," Xander said.

"The Aura are circling the wagons, so to speak, and we've had several families looking to relocate to the area. We'll be busy getting them settled and assuring them that Langsmith is still a safe place to live," Hendrex said.

"For someone no longer in a leadership position, you still act like it," Jaq snorted.

Hendrex rolled his eyes at Jaq. "Says the self-appointed leader of the merry band of woe is me. I can't publicly endanger my people without consequences."

Jaq flicked off his cousin, and Tyr couldn't help but smile at the family dynamics at play. It was clear Hendrex didn't get along well with his brother or his cousin, but the love was still there.

"Alright, before this meeting drags on longer than necessary, I think we've accomplished what we set out to do. We know what happened, and we all have plans to mitigate the fallout. If anything else comes up, we can meet again. Until then, know that I have eyes and ears everywhere," Tyr said.

With his thoughts stated and a goal in mind, Tyr stood and left the warehouse. He still wasn't entirely sure what was going on, but once he got back into his own territory and had a chance to record things, he may have a better idea of what his next move would be. In the meantime, he would take a page out of the Aura handbook and circle the wagons. A member of the Vampire Council had been attacked in Langsmith. The Vampires weren't going to take that lightly. The last thing anyone needed was an all-out war in Langsmith.

Cold Comfort

Gasping for air, Ruling Three leaned against the cool stonework of the human side of the Garden Gate. The trip was much worse than the last time, a sign he needed to get this meeting with Maximus over with and get back to completing his mission.

Ruling Three kicked the large parcel at his feet. Maybe it was lugging the dead weight that made the journey so rough. Either way, he needed to get it together quick. He promised Maximus an Aura more powerful than Disrayan to make up for his men losing her. That was a tall order outside of the Sanctuary of Ceres.

The opportunity to solve two major problems presented itself during the last joint effort to stabilize the Barrier crystal. Ruling One had passed out and the Security Force officers on duty were too exhausted to protest when he offered to take her to her private tent.

It was late in Ceres; the streets of Magelor had been silent. Ruling One, the frail old woman, had exhausted her energy in an attempt to show herself worthy of re-election. A necessary effort considering he had successfully coerced the people to move the elections to later that week. Too bad, word would travel she had passed out and then disappeared. It wasn't uncommon for elder Aura to wander off alone when it was close to their time. Ruling Three had been sure to leave a note expressing just that before he wrapped her in a woven blanket and spirited her away.

Now, he just needed to get her to Maximus and return to Ceres before anyone noticed he too was missing. His plan only worked if everyone continued to believe he hadn't set foot outside of the Great Sanctuary in years.

Gathering his strength, Ruling Three hefted Ruling One over his shoulder and made his way down the back alleys to the meeting spot he set with Maximus. He would hand Ruling One over to Maximus' men and be done with them both.

A black SUV pulled to the curb, and the driver rolled his window down.

"Toss her in the back and get in."

Ruling Three tensed.

"I'm just here to hand off my final delivery," Ruling Three said.

The Vampire smirked and shook his head.

"Don't make this harder than it needs to be, old man. Get in the back."

With a sigh, he opened the back door and tossed Ruling One onto the seat. He briefly contemplated making a run for it, but his energy was too depleted from the crossing for him to put up much of a fight, and he was no match for Vampire speed. He climbed into the car and made a silent prayer to the gods that he made it through this meeting with Maximus in one piece and not in the bonds of blood slavery.

When they arrived at Maximus' mansion, the men took over carrying Ruling One. Ruling Three had been forced to use more of his energy to keep her sedated on the long drive. He hated being this vulnerable in such a dangerous situation. His level of energy knowledge was the only ace up his sleeve. Without it, he was in just as much danger from Maximus and his men as an Auraless child. The only saving grace—the Vampires would be none the wiser to his weakened state. They could only tell the potency of his energy if he used it on them, or Horus forbid, they got a sample of his blood.

"Glad you could make it," Maximus said, taking a sip from his glass.

The liquid inside left a red tint to his lips and Ruling Three shuddered at the thought of the source who provided it. He could feel the Aura energy from here— fresh, vibrant, and horrifyingly familiar.

"I have come to end our association. I no longer need your assistance, and this last delivery should cancel my debt to you."

Ruling Three wanted out of there as soon as possible. Nothing in his plans involved becoming a Vampire snack, and he could easily see that being the outcome of this unplanned adventure deep into enemy territory.

Maximus scoffed.

"On the contrary. Your debt is far from paid. You have cost me not one but two prize pieces for my collection, and I'm afraid my confidence in you is greatly diminished."

"Two? How? What do you mean?"

"It doesn't matter. Your debt is not done, by far. You promised me a powerful young Aura female, and yet you have brought me a crone so depleted, her blood probably tastes of grave dirt."

Ruling Three shrugged. "I'm not familiar with either delicacy, so I will have to take your word for it."

Maximus surged from his seated position, red rage dancing in the deep, black pits of his soulless eyes.

"You dare mock me!"

Maximus' men moved forward and grabbed Ruling Three by the arms. He struggled against them, but it was of no use. Maximus pressed a sharpened letter opener against his throat. The blade stung like ice as it pricked his skin and drew blood. Both Vampires holding him tensed further at the smell of fresh blood.

Maximus pressed the letter opener deeper into Ruling Three's neck but not enough to cause permanent damage.

"Your arrogance outweighs the power you claim to have. Let's see what other secrets you may be keeping, Aura," Maximus snarled.

The opener gone, Maximus struck, his fangs worse than the pierce of the knife. Like hot pokers straight from the belly of the metal workers kiln. Ruling Three jerked and struggled like a fish on a line, desperate for release. Maximus drained him almost to the point of collapse and when he finally let go, Ruling Three knew he'd made a huge miscalculation.

"Please," he begged, but it was of no use. He could see in Maximus' eyes that this was the end.

"I left a little snack for you both, a bonus for your service during last night's fiasco. When you're done, go find me more," Maximus said before turning his back on Ruling Three and leaving him alone with two hungry Vampire thugs.

Ruling Three closed his eyes and began to pray again. Not for salvation, but for a quick and peaceful end.

.....

Enora smiled and shook her head as she awoke to her three best friends still sleeping on their respective spaces in her living room. It had been years since anything like this had happened. The last time had been shortly after graduating Security Force training. Only, instead of in a downtown condo, it had been in Disrayan's grandparents' tent.

Enora yawned and stretched her back and neck; at least, she had snagged the couch to sleep on. The others would have a hell of a time with their backs today. At least Enora's energy felt more stable and whole. Yesterday had been eye opening for her. She wondered if that's how Auraless people felt, knowing the energy was there, able to feel it but not access it. It was maddening.

"Wake up!"

Enora shook Disrayan awake since she was the closest to her. Disrayan was a light sleeper. The others would jump right up once Disrayan decided it was time for them to be. She groaned and slowly stretched awake.

"When did we fall asleep?"

"No idea, but it's about time for us to get back to evacuee duty," she answered after checking her phone.

Enora would have to go by her day job and show her face there first before disappearing to help with the evacuees. It was crazy to think there even were evacuees from Ceres, even if it was only a voluntary evacuation at this point. She went to her room to change, leaving Disrayan to handle waking the others. It was time to put her life back together. Last night was the one and only time she would let her emotions get the best of her. No more crying, no more bad boy shenanigans at her place of work, and most certainly no more talk of feelings with Jaquis Andromeda.

The girls were gone by the time she came down the stairs again. Which was fine because she didn't feel like facing the questions she forbade them from asking last night. She knew they would ask when they were alone again. She needed today to be a little slice of normal so she could continue to build her walls again. There was too much at stake for her to be off her game right now.

"You look like you got a good night's sleep," Detective Burns said as soon as Enora walked into the morgue.

She smiled and nodded.

"Yeah, got to bed earlier. You, however, look positively drained."

He nodded and took a long swig from his coffee cup.

"Yeah, I wanted to speak with you personally about something that's been bugging me about this last spurt of cases," he said.

Enora nodded and gestured for him to follow her to her office where they could chat relatively privately. Not that there were tons of people hanging around the morgue, live ones at least. Judging by the haggard look Detective Burns wore, it was best there were as minimal ears to overhear as possible.

"So, what's on your mind?" She took a seat at her desk and clasped her hands on the desk.

He eyed her before pulling out a stack of case files.

"These are just a few of the cases whose cause of death didn't add up," he said.

"You want me to look over them and see if the examining ME was mistaken?"

Enora reached for the cases. She didn't recognize any of the names, but she knew the faces the moment she saw them. It was the three fang-bangers who hadn't survived their transition. Her official cause of death was alcohol poisoning, but obviously, Detective Burns wasn't buying that one bit.

"Oh, I see."

She honestly couldn't blame him. From what Farrah had told her, the crime scene had been a blood bath, and clean-up crews hadn't been quick enough to beat the human cops to the scene. Once again, the Vampire population's recklessness in Langsmith forced her to lie to a respected colleague.

"Is that all you have to say? Enora, if you are in some kind of trouble, I can help you. I saw that thug hanging around yesterday." She stiffened at his use of the word thug.

"Jaq is not a thug, and if you think I would jeopardize my career over a man, then you have poor people reading skills," she snapped and handed him back the case files.

"I know alcohol poisoning didn't kill these boys," Detective Burns said, standing.

He positioned his body to be intimidating, but Enora wasn't buying the act.

"I don't know what you think is going on here, but I stand by every one of my medical conclusions. Now, if you are done being a paranoid ass hat, please leave my office."

Detective Burns stared her down before sucking his teeth and leaving. Enora waited a few seconds after he left before she sat back and let out a sigh of relief. Detective Burns wasn't the first officer to confront her about her autopsy findings, and he certainly wouldn't be the last if the Vampires continued to be such vile predatory bastards. Sadly, that was their nature and part of the reason she had her job in the first place.

A single tear ran down her cheek, and Enora quickly wiped it away. Maybe once the Barrier issue was settled, she would request a new position on the Security Force, one with much less death and deception. For now, she had two bodies to look over before she could head over to the gate and help with the evacuees. She wished she had something less depressing to look forward to that evening. Her mind focused on the one thing sure to brighten her mood. Her hand reached for her phone but she stopped when she immediately scrolled to Jaq's number.

"No, no. That's not what you need, girl," she chastised herself before shoving her phone back into her purse.

With a sigh, she stood, slid on her lab coat, and headed into the cold room. At least today's customers hadn't come from some gruesome crime scene. An elderly couple found in an old vacation cabin. Since no one had reported them missing, they still needed to be examined to ensure there was no foul play involved. Enora hoped it was a simple case of old age.

"Holy shit!" she cursed as she unzipped the first bag.

She was not prepared for the desiccated body that greeted her. Not because of its dried-out state that made it look almost mummified, but because she recognized the face and braided crown of grey hair. The lone tear she flicked away earlier became many more as she rushed from the room. She made it to the bathroom in time to heave the piece of dry toast she'd grabbed on her way out the door.

"Dr. Circinus, are you okay?" her coworker called through the bathroom door.

Enora forced herself upright and went to wash her hands. As much as it pained her, there was no way she would be passing this case off to someone else. Ruling One deserved a proper send off, and it was Enora's job to ensure that it happened without human interference. She cleaned her face and straightened her lab coat before leaving the restroom.

"I'm fine, thank you," she said and went back to work.

If her initial reaction was one of grief, her next anger. Ruling One had obviously not died of natural causes, and the proof was right there on the curve between her neck and shoulder. Two evenly spaced puncture wounds just below a shallow cut.

"Fucking Vampires."

.....

The last thing Jaq expected was to see Enora lingering in the doorway of The Resistance's unofficial headquarters. She kept her head low as she leaned against the wall outside the private event room at the coffee shop The Resistance frequented now that Club Obelisk was no longer a safe space to hang out.

"Just give me a second," Jaq said to the man he'd been talking to.

It didn't matter that it was a serious discussion of the man's concerns. The only concern Jaq had was for Enora in that moment. He approached her slowly before pulling her into his arms. He knew something was seriously wrong when she didn't even attempt to protest or pull away, only sinking into his embrace. Her body shook with silent sobs. He glanced into the other room and noticed they were drawing attention, so he slowly guided her back into the public side of the coffee shop.

He signaled for the barista to bring them some tea as he settled in with her on one of the cozy couches in the corner.

"Shh, it's okay. Whatever happened. We will make sure that everything is okay."

Enora looked at him, her eyes swollen and red with tears but dancing with rage at the same time.

"They killed Ruling One," she hissed.

Her words were a shot of ice through his veins. He stiffened and raised an eyebrow.

"Who did what now?"

"Fucking Vamps somehow got to Ruling One. Her body came to the morgue today. I almost..." She choked back another sob and sank against his shoulder.

Jaq rubbed her back and placed a kiss on her forehead.

"Have you called Donovan?"

Enora shook her head. "I was going to tell him in person. I didn't trust myself to get it out over the phone, and then, instead of finding Donovan, I ended up here."

"You came to me first?"

She nodded again.

Jaq couldn't help the way that made his heart swell. In her time of distress, her body instinctively brought her to him. She sought him out for comfort, instead of pure distraction. It was a step in the right direction. Maybe his declaration of love the other day hadn't fallen entirely on deaf ears, wasn't as one sided as she wanted him to believe. Still, her news couldn't have come at a worse time. Ruling One was dead, and not just dead, drained by Vampires. That was an act of war. One that couldn't go without retaliation of some kind.

While Jaq comforted Enora, he sent an emergency text letting Donovan know what happened, and then another to his second to let her know that shit had hit the fan. He wasn't surprised when they both immediately replied that they were on it. That allowed him to relax and give his woman the comfort she needed. Hell, the comfort they both needed. Jaq railed against the system all day. He thought it was antiquated and detrimental to the overall survival of his people. That didn't mean he didn't feel the loss of such a respected Aura as any true Aura should. An elder as great as Ruling One deserved a better end than draining by Vampire. Regardless of her political isolationist stance.

The barista arrived with their tea, and Jaq held Enora in his lap until she was calm enough to slide onto the cushions next to him. He felt her gathering her strength and building her walls back up. His mood worsened at the thought of her pulling away, only she didn't. She took his hand in hers before reaching for the cup of tea. She took a few sips and straightened her spine.

"Thank you," she whispered.

"Anytime, love. You know I am here for you always."

She gave him a look that would cut anyone to the quick, but its impact was softened by the fact she still held his hand, her thumb rubbing softly over his finger.

"I shouldn't have come here. I don't want to interfere with your life," she said and tried to stand, but he pulled her back into his lap.

"You came to exactly the right place. You've had an impossible few days. It's only natural you would seek comfort with your boy-friend."

"Boyfriend? Look, Jaq, we—"

He didn't let her finish her sentence. He pressed his lips to hers, swallowing her words. She tensed before melting into him, her soft tongue slipping into his mouth to tease and torment him. Torment, considering he couldn't expand on her sexual foray out here in pub-lic. Besides, as much as he would love to distract her with his dick, now wasn't the time. She was emotionally distraught, and he didn't want to take advantage of her in that way.

She needed to see another side of him. The side truly in love with her. That saw no other woman since Enora let Jaq into her life. Truly cared about her day when he asked. You know, relationship stuff. Forever kind of stuff. He pulled away, both of them breathless and bothered.

"Finish your tea, right now isn't the time for the discussion we need to have."

Enora looked as if she would protest but instead, finished her tea quietly and stood to leave.

"I need to go. I'm supposed to be helping with evacuees."

Jaq nodded and stood as well.

"I'll come with you. If the Vampires are killing Aura, you shouldn't be out on your own."

"I'll be fine. I'm overthinking this. Ruling One might have come to see how the Aura outside the Barrier were doing after the surge and ran across a rogue Vampire who was also affected. I heard there have been more rabid Vamps since the surge as well."

Jaq knew she was in denial of things. They both knew Ruling One would never willingly leave Ceres for any reason. And if for some miracle she had, she was far too powerful to be overcome by a rabid street Vamp. Even if they caught her off-guard initially. Nothing about what they knew to be true about One's death added up to anything good. Somehow, someway, the Vamps had found a way into Ceres, or worse, had an Aura working for them who was powerful enough to disarm Ruling One and get her out of Ceres undetected.

There were only three Aura powerful enough to do that, and only one with the balls and the motive to do so. Combined with the fact that Jaq already knew a powerful Aura had been at the Vampire Council member's death mansion, left Jaq with only one conclusion. The traitor was a member of the former Ruling Council, and it wasn't too far of a stretch to figure out who that might be. Damn the consequences. If Jaq caught Ruling Three before the Security Force did, the man was dead.

.....

Enora knew it was a bad idea to just show up at a resistance hang out on the off-chance Jaq was there. Hell, it was stupid of her to go to him in the first place when she really needed to take her ass to Ceres and report to the proper authorities. Still, when he'd pulled her into his arms and held her while she cried, her heart had opened to him in a way she had resisted for so long.

He'd shown her a different side of himself at the coffee shop.

64

To be honest, she'd been there longer than he knew. She'd hung out in the back watching as he did his thing. Floating around the room, oozing masculine charm and charisma. He reassured worried teens, had enlightened and open discussions with men and women of different supernatural abilities about the fate of Langsmith. If it hadn't been a group of whiny rebels calling themselves a movement, Enora could almost see Jaq in a position with the Ruling Council. They all knew he was powerful enough as an Andromeda.

It was because of how she saw him in this new light that she welcomed his embrace when he'd finally come to her. Took the comfort he offered and didn't protest when he practically carried her to the couch out front and ordered her tea.

"It really wasn't necessary for you to come with me," she said for the third time as he drove her in his SUV to the factory where the Gate to Ceres was hidden.

He smirked and pressed a kiss to the back of her hand. He hadn't let go of her hand since the coffee shop. If she didn't know better, it felt like he was even sharing a bit of his energy with her to help calm her nerves.

"I told you, I have business to attend to."

"Sure, you do," she said.

"You calling me a liar?"

His tone was a little harsh, but when she looked at him, he was still smiling, and there was a twinkle of mischief in his eyes.

"I'm saying that, however well-intentioned your concern, I am a grown ass woman capable of taking care of myself."

He sighed.

"I know that, Enora. I know damn well how smart, sexy, and independent you are. It's what draws me to you so strongly. Knowing you don't need me to take care of you at all. The issue here is I want to take care of you anyway, and you won't let me."

Enora pulled her hand from his, desperate to put any kind of space between them in the closed quarters of his SUV. The drive to the factory from downtown was a short one, but the last remaining block seemed like an eternity while he waited for her to respond. Honestly, she wasn't sure what to say to him.

"Hey, I think I've fallen for you, even though I've tried my

damnedest not to." Or "*why did you have to be so much more than the shallow man-child I thought you were and have an amazing dick game to boot?*"

Shaking her head, Enora decided to stare out the window. The awkward silence grew like a chasm between them. He reached for her hand again, and she let him take it.

"Like I said, we can talk about this later under better circumstances."

He pulled the car into a parking spot close to the factory and let go of her hand so he could get out and come around to help her out of the SUV. She rolled her eyes but allowed him to lift her from the car and set her on her feet. She thought he would let her go, but he crowded her body with his, pressing her against the passenger door.

"Jaq," she breathed, and he smiled before kissing her softly on the lips.

"If there is one thing you should know about me without me having to say it, I hate hiding who and what I am. That includes who I am with . I tried because I was so desperate for a chance with you, but you have to realize I am a man with needs, a human being with a heart that is just as easily broken as yours. So please, if you feel anything for me other than a love of how good my dick feels inside you, put me out of my misery. Let me be your man."

He pulled away and left her feeling breathless and guilty all at once. She leaned against his car for a moment longer before pulling herself together and heading for the staging area where techs were already frantically readying for the next arrival of evacuees.

"How are things going today?" she asked jumping right into the fray.

"The last family barely made it through. The grandmother was too weak to survive, and a pregnant mother had to be taken to a hospital to ensure her baby was okay," one of the techs replied.

She could see the fear and desperation in the other techs' eyes as the gate began to glow. The next evacuees would be arriving shortly, and it was obvious they were expecting the worst. Except, it wasn't a family to cross over. Hendrex, looking like death, collapsed to the ground after crossing. Enora rushed over, but Zazzie got to him first. She could feel her friend's energy as it flared before Zazzie connected with Hendrex and brought him back to the conscious world.

Enora helped Zazzie get Hendrex to the medical area for fluids. "What happened to the family?"

"They heard about Elder Grendwall and decided the trip wasn't worth the risk. I couldn't in good faith try to convince them otherwise, especially when I wasn't sure if even I could make this trip," he said.

Zazzie lovingly stroked his hair and murmured prayers of rejuvenation and health while the rest of Enora's team looked defeated. Enora wanted to focus on the task at hand, on cleaning for the day, since there was obviously not going to be another family for her to help, but then she remembered Jaq. She raced for the gate and started to draw the runes frantically, but her nerves kept her from doing them correctly.

"Enora, what's wrong?" Zazzie said, pulling her away from the wall.

Enora hadn't realized just how frantic she looked until she saw the concern in her friends' eyes and felt the tear streaming down her face.

"I—I..."

She didn't know how to explain without revealing more than she wanted to. So instead of admitting her fear about Jaq's well-being, she broke down and told her friend about Ruling One.

"I need to report it, they need to know."

Zazzie held her close and guided her away from the gate.

"Donovan has probably already contacted the Commander about this. There is no need for you to risk a trip into Ceres, especially with how the surge seems to be effecting you," Zazzie said.

The rational part of Enora understood that to be true. The other much less rational part screamed at her to go after Jaq. To make sure he had made it safely to the other side and wasn't too weakened by the trip not to make it back.

"I know, it's just..."

Enora recognized the signs of an anxiety attack building in her body, her limbs were tingly, and her breathing shallow and forced. Her mind raced with doom's day scenarios, but she couldn't pinpoint or fixate on any one thing.

"Shh, it's okay. You did your part, and now it's up to Donovan and the rest of the Security Force. "

Zazzie could feel Hendrex and Zazzie's concern flowing through her, calming her nerves. Giving in, she relaxed into the chair and took a few deep breaths to calm and center herself. Her anxiety slowly subsided, and when she finally refocused on the world around her, Farrah and Disrayan had arrived.

"I'm okay, guys, really I am. I just got overwhelmed."

They eyed her suspiciously before handing her a brown paper bag.

She rolled her eyes.

"I don't feel sick, and I'm not hyperventilating."

"Just take this with you to the bathroom," Disrayan said and shoved the bag into her hands.

Enora frowned.

"You don't think? No way! I'm not stupid. I've been careful."

"Yeah, yeah, just take the damn test," Farrah said, and Enora groaned before heading into the factory to the nearest restroom.

Of course, they followed her to the bathroom. She flicked her friends off as she went into the first stall. When she was done, she put the test on a paper towel on the sink and washed her hands.

"I would know if I was pregnant. Aura woman can feel the shift in their energy. It's not even possible. We used condoms. I'm on birth control." She was so busy rambling she missed Zazzie grabbing the test and raising an eyebrow at her.

"Well then, it's a solstice miracle. Congratulations, mama."

Enora froze and turned slowly to face her friends who all grinned from ear to ear.

"No way! That's....that isn't. The test is faulty. Maybe the surge messed with my hormones." Enora didn't want to believe it could be true.

"Okay, whatever. Now who's the lucky father-to-be?"

Enora bit her lip and shook her head.

"I need a moment," she said and ran from the restroom.

Reach

Jaq lay in the fake grass just in front of the Garden Gate, taking slow deep breaths while his body adjusted from the horrendous trip through the gate. It felt like he'd just marched a hundred miles carrying three hundred pounds on his back, all while his skin was being flayed by three hundred scalpels. He was hot and cold, numb but in excruciating pain. He had to close his eyes to avoid adding sensory overload to his list of ailments.

While he'd wanted to go straight to the Security Force office, he now needed to find one of Ceres's healers or he wouldn't make it home to Enora that night. Something he was determined to do now that he knew there was hope for them. He didn't want to give her too much time to put her walls up now that he'd gotten a peak at what lay behind them.

He forced himself to get up and walk slowly into Magelor. He was well aware of all the stares he garnered as he passed. Jaquis Andromeda was one infraction away from being an enemy of the state. He was a rogue, an outsider, a menace. Still, he held his head high as he walked through the maze of stalls. Taking note of just how much had changed in his childhood home. The purple sky had lost its vibrance, a low grayish fog hung over everything. A suffocating blanket of misplaced energy that wrapped around everything with an oppressive force.

The weather seemed to reflect the mood of the people Jaq passed. The normally cheerful Aura looked positively glum and unhappy. No one smiled or called out the customary greetings. None of the merchants beckoned him to check out their wares. It was chilling, like a scene out of a horror movie. He made his way to the inner circle of Magelor, random groups of people gathered around, whispers of discontent everywhere but not a word about Ruling One's passing.

Either word hadn't gotten to Ceres yet, or Commander Mars was keeping the information to himself for whatever reason. Well, for an obvious reason. With the atmosphere of Ceres so hostile, the last thing the people needed was more bad news.

"What are you doing here?"

Jaq turned to find his father standing behind him. Jaq hadn't seen his father in years. Not since the man found out Jaq was the leader of The Resistance and pretty much disowned him.

"What's it to you, old man?"

Grant Andromeda frowned. If it weren't for the short gray hair and thick lines of disapproval marring his otherwise youthful appearance, Jaq and his father would look almost identical. Same broad shoulders and slim athletic build. The strong Andromeda cheekbones and nose. If only sharing DNA helped people get along better.

"If you're here to stir more trouble, just leave now. As you can see, we don't need anyone stirring the pot," he said.

Jaq smirked.

"Don't worry about what I'm doing, old man. You gave up that right when you decided I wasn't your blood."

He walked away, leaving his dad sputtering. Jaq wished he could say it didn't hurt to have almost no relationship with his father, but it did. A lot. He pushed his way through the small crowd in front of the Meeting House door and waltzed right passed the Security Force Guards who tried to apprehend him before he could reach the Commander's office.

Commander Mars sat at his desk scowling over a stack of papers. He didn't look up from his paperwork when Jaq came in with several guards behind him.

"Jaquis Andromeda, to what do I owe this visit?" Commander Mars asked. He waved the guards away with an absent wave.

Jaq smirked at the grumbling guards and waited until they were gone before he spoke.

"I came to discuss what happened to Ruling One."

Commander Mars looked over his papers with a frown.

"Look, kid, it's a tragedy Ruling One was caught off-guard outside of Ceres. There is no need to go spreading unfounded conspiracy theories and getting everyone riled up," the Commander said.

"So, that's the story you're running with? We both know she couldn't have been overpowered by just any Vampire, and a Vampire that powerful wouldn't be roaming the streets of Langsmith for a bite. They have protocol for that."

"My job is to ensure the Secret of Ceres is safe. Ruling One's death was unfortunate, in both means and timing, but she is one Aura who would never cross that line. That makes it not my business. Now, I have an election to coordinate if you would show yourself out."

"You are really worried about elections right now? Those are weeks away, and Ceres is falling around your ears!"

Commander Mars tossed his paper work and glared at Jaq.

"Don't you raise your voice at me, Jaquis. You have been a pain in the ass for far too long to come waltzing in here like I can't just have you tried and exiled. As for the elections, as you are still for the moment eligible to participate, they have been moved to the end of this week. I literally have three days to get everything ready, so run along before I change my mind about letting you walk out of here."

Jaq frowned at the commander but didn't argue. He knew it was pointless. Commander Mars was set in the old ways. Even if the commander had helped Hendrex in his time of need, Jaq knew his affinity for the Andromeda clan did not extend to him.

Jaq left the Meeting House but couldn't help making his presence felt in Ceres. He found the largest group of people outside of Ceres and got their attention by standing right in the middle of them.

"Listen, I don't know what bullshit the Security Force and others are spewing, but I'm going to tell y'all the truth whether you believe me or not. Ceres is rotting from the inside out. Politics and power have corrupted or blinded the current leadership, and Ruling One is dead. The Barrier is beyond repair, and travel through the gate to the human world is barely survivable at this point. Your choices are clear as day, and yet, you refuse to see them. Leave Ceres now before you get taken with it, either when the Barrier falls or when the shitheads in charge run the place into the ground. It's your choice."

He didn't wait for them to respond. He marched out of Magelor and to the Garden Gate. Taking a deep breath and shaking out his shoulders, he prepared for the painful trip back. The entire way, the only thing that kept him going was the thought of Enora waiting for him on the other side. It wasn't until he pushed through and found not a soul on the other side that he almost let the pain overcome him. Yet, the gate hadn't closed behind him. People had followed him from Ceres. A couple of teenagers fell through the gate, one on top of the other, shaking and crying out in pain.

"Shit," Jaq cursed.

The techs and volunteers had cleared out for the night. There was no one there to help them, or so he thought. Movement in the periphery caught his attention before Sarah, Tyr's adopted daughter and personal fly on the wall, emerged from the shadows.

"I sent word that help was needed. Jasmine will be here shortly," Sarah then curled her body around the pile of sick Aura and started to purr.

It took Jaq a moment to realize it was the cat Shifter's way of trying to help, trying to comfort them. Even as shitty as he felt, he couldn't be upstaged by the Shifter teen, so he got down on the ground and huddled with them until help arrived. So much for getting home to Enora that evening. His night would be full with getting the teenagers settled until the morning.

.....

The Langsmith cemetery felt different during the day. The large trees that dotted the vast grounds weren't casting ominous shadows or whispering menacingly with the pleas of the less fortunate. In the daylight hours, it was actually quite peaceful. Enora needed peaceful at the moment. The dual bombshell of losing Ruling One and possibly becoming a mother was too much for her to adequately process in the presence of others. She would deal with one thing at a time. The first being ensuring Ruling One's spirit remained at rest.

Enora had placed a rush order for the cremation of Ruling One's remains and now carried her ashes across the rows of headstones to the back of the cemetery. The large "family plot" the Aura had purchased to intern the bodies and ashes of their kind. There was a low wrought iron fence that surrounded the plot. No large gravestones were placed in this area. Only rows of wooden crosses wrapped in various flowers and herbs to keep the area clear of evil spirits and to aid in the passage to the afterlife of those whose ashes and bodies were placed there. In the middle of the plot stood a large oak tree.

Enora laid her blanket beneath the tree to meditate and help those who were having trouble crossing. It seemed like ages since she was last there. Even though it had only been a few days. The night of the energy surge. She wondered how many restless spirits were running amok since that fateful night.

Enora sat cross-legged on the blanket and set the urn next to her candle. She should have waited until the night when it was easier to work with the dead. She just didn't have the time. She needed to do this and get back to helping at the gate.

Settling, she attempted to clear her mind. Picturing the leaves above her head dancing on the wind. Letting her thoughts float by but not entertaining them, no matter how tempting or triggering. Her breathing slowed and deepened. Once she felt her body relaxing, Enora let her energy creep out like tiny tendrils or feelers. Searching out any restless spirits lingering in the area. Even if she encountered those who wished to do her harm, they couldn't reach her here. This section of the cemetery was protected.

What she found made her blood run cold.

Help us!

The voices shouted almost in unison, creating a cacophony of sound inside her head. It was almost enough to knock her out of her trance. So many elders had been sent to their graves because of the surge. Enora hadn't even known there were that many outside the Barrier. There was no way she could guide them all individually. To make matters worse, there were many other supernatural as well, Vampires and Shifters of all kinds. The Shifters were older, like the Aura elders she came across, but as for the Vampires, she couldn't be certain. She only knew their deaths had to have been violent, otherwise their spirits would have crossed immediately upon their passing.

Most Vampires had already experienced death once before, so they knew exactly how to get to the afterlife without help. Only those who were not satisfied with how they died lingered. The fact that there were so many was surprising, to say the least. They hadn't been there before and would have had to die in town for her to reach their spirits. Not knowing exactly what the surge was or how it occurred, she took a mental note to add that Vampires hadn't been immune or somehow fortified to its effects either.

Enora concentrated her focus on the urn in front of her. Using the ashes inside as a beacon for Ruling One's spirit. If she had already passed, then Enora would feel nothing, but if she wandered, it would draw her to Enora.

"My child." Ruling One's spirit found her almost immediately.

"I have told the others of your passing. Your death shall not go unsolved."

"I am grateful, but that is not the only thing tying me here."

"What more is there?"

"A great evil still lurks. Threatening everything the Aura are and will be."

"Great evil?"

"The one responsible for my death."

"Who?"

"I will lead the others to the final resting place. You, my child, take care, and remember, a life without hope and love is no life at all."

Ruling One's spirit departed in a flash of light so bright Enora would have shielded her eyes if they weren't already closed. The light lingered, drawing to it the spirits of lingering Aura. Enora watched as they formed a line and stepped into the light. Similar to the crossing at the Garden Gate.

It made Enora wonder.

Was the afterlife just another dimensional pocket like Ceres? Could she access the afterlife the same as she did the space between?

As soon as the last Aura crossed, the light began to fade. Enora could feel the spirits of the Shifters moving cautiously toward the light.

Go! Be free!

They didn't need any further encouragement. A few even shifted to their animal forms before bounding through the gate. The Vampires came next, as if in pursuit of the Aura and Shifters who had just crossed. As the first Vampire came near, the white light turned red and became a ring of flame. The Vampires screamed as the ring chased them; those caught by it burned into neat piles of ash on the concrete.

Enora couldn't stand to see anymore. She may not be friendly with Vampires, but that didn't mean she wished anyone the torment of the underworld. Still, she didn't want to risk forcing herself out of the trance too soon. So, instead of focusing on outer spirits, she turned her energy inward. More specifically, to her abdomen where she searched for any hint of additional energy. It would be too early for there to be much, but from stories she'd overheard from expectant Aura mothers, their pregnancies were confirmed viable once there was an additional source of energy detected within them.

Some mothers even claimed to be able to communicate with their babies when connecting with their energy. Enora searched and searched but found nothing. Not a single spark or unknown anything within her. A warm tear fell down her cheek, then another. She broke her trance and wiped them away. Human tests were faulty. Maybe she wasn't pregnant after all, or if she was, it was probably too early for her to connect with the baby's energy.

More tears fell from her eyes, running down her cheeks and dripping from her chin. Enora didn't bother trying to fight the wave of sadness and fear that struck her. She was alone in a safe place. If there was ever a time where she could vent, now was the time. She uncrossed her legs and lay flat on the blanket. Staring at the blue sky that slowly turned dark as the sun began to set for the evening. She couldn't wallow in her emotions for long, but she needed this time.

She settled in a different kind of trance. One where her mind did its best to solve the issues of the day. Her possible pregnancy, what that would mean for her relationship with Jaq. How exactly had Ruling One fallen prey to Vampires and what her death would mean for the upcoming Council elections? Her thoughts were interrupted by the buzzing of her phone in her pocket.

Sitting up, Enora wiped the tears from her face and pulled out her phone. She expected it to be one of the girls, Zazzie, more specifically, calling to check on her. It wasn't that Farrah and Disrayan wouldn't care, they just weren't as emotionally in tune as Zazzie. Instead, it was Donovan. What little progress Enora had made in calming herself was ripped away as soon as she read Donovan's message. She was needed again. The Vampires had attacked The Resistance.

.....

Jaq was just getting the teens settled in at his apartment when his phone began to ring. He was so exhausted he contemplated letting it go to voicemail, but when it kept ringing and ringing, he finally answered.

"Yeah?" he barked, but his attitude changed as soon as he heard the frantic voice on the other line.

"The clubhouse has been compromised," was all he heard before a loud scream followed by a feral growl.

His blood ran cold as he raced out of his apartment. Phone still in hand, he called for backup. Donovan, Mack, and Hendrex all arrived as he did. The youth center eerily silent. Donovan grabbed his arm when he tried to go through the front door.

"Hey, I know you want to go in guns blazing, but we need to be smart about this," he hissed.

Jaq sighed and ran a hand over his face. "Sure, man, sure."

Mack clapped him on the back as they huddled to make a plan. They would go in through the back, since that was closer to the area The Resistance had deemed the clubhouse. They rounded the building cautiously, but when they reached the back and found a Vampire feeding directly from a young Aura male, Jaq lost it. He rushed forward, pulling the Vampire away, and he began to wail on him.

It didn't matter that the Vampire was more physically powerful, Jaq's adrenaline and energy knowledge boosted his ability to keep the Vampire down. He barely registered Hendrex helping the young Aura get away while Mack and Donovan pushed their way inside.

"Jaq! That's enough!" Hendrex's voice called out to him, but Jaq didn't stop. Couldn't stop. He wanted to kill the bastard more than he wanted to see what carnage lay before them inside.

Hendrex stepped in and pulled Jaq off the bloody Vampire. Jaq had no idea how long he'd been beating the Vampire, but it had been long enough for Xander, Claude, and Greg to arrive. Even knowing they were friends and had nothing to do with this attack, Jaq couldn't look at them without getting angry all over again.

He wiped his bloody fists on his pants and took off running down the alley. He couldn't stay and see any more of this. He needed to chill out and get his head together. He walked to the end of the alley and back until he heard voices coming from inside the Youth Center. He nearly broke down when he realized it was Jasmine helping Donovan and Mack instruct the survivors out of the building. *There were survivors*, he told himself. Not just the boy he pulled the Vampire off of, but at least ten more. All saved by the contingency plan that he had set in place for just such a scenario.

No one should rail against the system as openly as they did without planning for some form of retaliation. He couldn't shake that they had lost people. Most likely, those who were new to the group, who hadn't been fully initiated and gone through the training. When they started to file out the door, Jaq rushed forward, catching an upset and exhausted Jasmine in his arms. He held her close as she cried into his shoulders.

"Thank Horus, you're okay," he said, and she laughed a little through her tears.

"What? You thought I couldn't handle myself?"

He shook his head and squeezed her tighter.

"I should have been here with you," he said.

"Nah, you were getting those kids settled at your place. You were where you were supposed to be," she said, but Jaq didn't miss the flash of sadness in her eyes.

"Who is missing?"

She shook her head.

"We can figure that out later. Right now, I'm just glad to still be breathing and to have saved as many as I could. They weren't trying to capture us. It was like watching a feeding frenzy on shark week the way they swarmed us and..." She didn't finish what she was saying as her eyes found something more interesting behind him.

Jaq followed her gaze, and his eyes collided with Enora. She had obviously just arrived, her bag still tucked firmly under her arm. She shot daggers at him and Jasmine, who was still in his arms. Guiltily, he let her go and made a move toward Enora. He wanted to set things straight. To tell her it wasn't like that, but she had already moved on. Setting down her bag, she got to work tending to the wounded and making transportation arrangements for those who were not.

Jaq watched her and noticed how different she carried herself than before. She appeared drained, her shoulders slumped, her face drawn with deep shadows under her eyes that were puffy and red as if she had spent all day crying. He wanted to respect that she was working and that others needed her right now, but he couldn't not go to her.

"Enora," he said blocking her path.

She tried to move around him without saying a word, but he grabbed her arm and held her in place.

"Let go of me before you make a scene," Enora hissed, and the venom in her voice combined with the questioning stares of the injured around them made him drop her arm and let her go.

"We will talk later," he said before heading to where Donovan and Hendrex huddled together speaking.

"This isn't good. The Vampires have never openly attacked like this before," Donovan said.

"Do you think it's because of the raids on the monster houses?"

"Possibly, but it doesn't make sense that they would just attack and not try to capture anyone to make up for the ones we saved."

"Either way, this is an act of war. Regardless of if Ceres decides to do anything, The Resistance is now on full alert," Jaq said breaking into their conversation.

Donovan shook his head.

"The last thing we need is for you to go retaliating and making a bigger mess of things. This event was tragic, but with the surge making everyone and everything so skittish, it could just be a couple of rogues looking for what they thought would be easy targets."

"What are we doing guessing about this? Why not ask the asshole over there?" Jaq pointed to the Vampire he'd been beating a few moments before. "He should be healed enough to talk again."

"He's not going to talk after you went all caveman on him," Hendrex sighed.

"He will if he knows what's good for him. He's lucky he only got a physical beating. He hasn't felt what I can do with my energy yet," Jaq said and started to march over, but Greg stepped into his path.

"Why don't you go check in with Tyr? I noticed some of the injured were Shifters. I'll interrogate the Vampire."

Jaq eyed the man before nodding and backing away. It was probably for the best. Jaq would probably kill the guy before he got any useful information out of him, and while he had a bit of an issue with trusting a Vampire to interrogate a Vampire, maybe the asshole would be more open to questions from his own kind. Honestly, for Jaq it didn't matter what the blood sucker had to say. What happened tonight was an act of war, a war the Vampires had started with the wrong group of supernaturals. The Resistance would not take this lying down.

.....

Sarah watched Enora as she made her way through the cemetery. Darting from tree to tree in her cat form, Sarah did her best to avoid detection. She knew she should be at The Resistance headquarters, but somehow, as soon as she had scented Jaq's mate earlier that day, she had become immediately protective. She felt an inexplicable urge to stick by her side and make sure nothing happened to her. Maybe it was because of her pregnancy.

A Shifter's instinct was always to protect the future of their pack. Jaquis Andromeda and Enora weren't Shifters, but Jaq was pack to Tyr. That made Jaq and his mate pack to Sarah. The pack had information that the Vampires had mobilized for something on the night of the surge. Maybe for the source of the surge. If anyone was going to figure out where that massive energy blast came from, it would be the Aura.

Enora worked with the dead. Such an odd thing for a woman who appeared to be so sweet and shy. Death had a way of corrupting people. Like a darkness that clung to their soul. Sarah had dealt with her fair share of death before coming to the Langsmith pack. Maybe that was why Sarah was so intrigued by Enora over the others. They dealt with the darkness, but Enora had found a way to hide from it. A skill Sarah so desperately wanted to learn.

The briny scent of tears tickled Sarah's nostrils, and she tightened her grip on the tree branch above Enora to keep from shifting back to human form and revealing herself. Sarah wasn't exactly hidden, a big black cat in a tree in broad daylight. Her only camouflage was the thick cover of leaves that hadn't yet fallen from the tree's branches. In fact, this tree felt different than the others. Despite it being well into fall, the leaves still held their bright green color while the others were already turning varying shades of reds and golden yellow.

This entire section of the cemetery was alive. Sarah's cat could feel the magic radiating from the ground as soon as she breached the wrought iron fence. It traveled over her fur like a soft caress. Her cat almost purred with how good it felt. So different from Sarah's encounters with Aura energy in the past. It usually felt like being zapped by static electricity.

The energy intensified as Enora performed some sort of ritual to connect with the dead. Sarah moved farther up the tree to avoid being detected. She wasn't sure how she would explain her presence if she was caught. The energy around them shifted and changed to something less calming, to something more frantic. An immense sadness overwhelmed Sarah, causing tears to well in her eyes, even in cat form.

She watched as Enora lay staring at the sky. She was too lost in thought to notice Sarah just above her in the tree. Sarah felt wrong for intruding on the obviously private moment. She began to retreat, forcing her cat away from Enora to the other side of the tree. She could leap from that side of the tree to the other side of the fence without being detected. She was just about to make the leap when her ears detected the buzz of Enora's phone.

Sarah hesitated, waiting to see if it was a phone call. It wasn't, but the anguished expression on Enora's face sealed the deal for Sarah. She couldn't leave her now. Sarah couldn't shake the sense that this woman was in danger. It was the same fear that had lead her to following her friend Disrayan until she discovered the Vampire's plans.

Enora frantically grabbed her things and ran from the cemetery. It made it more difficult for Sarah to follow without being caught by Enora or one of the few humans lingering this late in the cemetery to pay their respects. It took every ounce of Sarah's training to keep to the shadows, jumping from tombstone to tombstone until Enora reached her car. At that point, Sarah had to let her go. She could track her later. Sarah found the tree where she had stashed her backpack and shifted back to human form.

She quickly got dressed and tossed her pack on her shoulders. She noticed the indicator light on her phone flashing and took the time to check her messages. Her blood ran cold as she saw the message from The Resistance phone chain. No wonder Enora had run. The Resistance had been attacked by Vampires. As much as Sarah wanted to go to the scene, she knew she needed to check in with Tyr first. He had already left three messages for her, his tone morphing gradually from pissed off Alpha to concerned parent. The Shifter compound would be her first stop, and after she calmed Tyr and Sequoia of their fears, she would head back out to finish her job.

"Where the hell have you been?" Tyr stood on the porch of the cabin; his arms crossed over his chest when Sarah arrived home.

"I was following a lead. I was shifted, so I didn't have my phone on me," she said.

"No excuse, young lady. Get your butt in this house," Sequoia snapped.

Sarah hadn't seen her standing behind Tyr. He was in full Alpha mode, meaning he would be on red alert when it came to his mate

Sequoia. Sarah bowed her head and did as told. She was grateful for Tyr and Sequoia taking her in as one of their own. Still, she had lived so long without parental guidance it was hard for her to deal when they both got like this. Tyr was a little better about working with her, but Sequoia had stepped into full mom mode as soon as Sarah had agreed to let them adopt her.

"Sorry," Sarah grumbled.

Sequoia pulled her into a hug before she could step through the door.

"We were so worried. The Vampires are attacking Shifters. I don't know what I would do if anything happened to you," Sequoia said.

Sarah hugged her back and sighed.

"I'm sorry I worried you. I'm safe. I'm here with you."

"Damn straight, you're here, and you will be staying here until the threat is over," Tyr barked.

Sarah moved out of Sequoia's grasp to glare at Tyr.

"I have a job to do. I can't just hide out here."

"A job I assigned to you that I am now suspending until it is safe. Your new assignment is to stay here in the cabin with Sequoia," Tyr said.

Sarah bristled as she felt the full force of his Alpha charisma. Tyr had never used it against her before, mostly because he never had to before. Tyr had saved her from the streets, had cared for her like his own cub even before he mated Sequoia. Sarah bit her lip and marched into the living room of the cabin.

"Yes, Alpha," she said.

Sequoia grabbed Tyr's arm and dragged him to the other room.

"You didn't need to use your Alpha voice on her," Sequoia spat.

Sarah smirked. At least, Sequoia had her back in that regard.

"I know, I just. I got too worked up and didn't realize."

Sarah felt a little better about the situation knowing Tyr regretted his actions. However, it didn't matter. Alpha voice or not, Sarah's defective status also made her immune to Alpha power. She could feel it, for sure, but she wasn't susceptible to the automatic obedience it spawned in others. Looking back, it was probably for that reason her original pack left her for dead as a kitten. Being a runt who could barely shift was one thing, being a barely shifting runt who couldn't be controlled by the Alpha was another.

Tyr and Sequoia's argument was cut short by Tyr's phone ringing. Sarah knew exactly what it was about. If Shifters were being attacked, Tyr would need to respond. Once he was gone, Sequoia came back into the living room and sat on the couch with her. She tried not to look antsy as Sequoia forced her to watch a cheesy family sitcom with her. As soon as the credits were done, Sarah excused herself to her room. Sequoia gave her a sad look and kissed her forehead before nodding that it was okay.

Her next actions were surely going to get her in a crap ton of trouble, but Sarah couldn't help herself. She was driven by some force inside her to find Enora. To protect her from whatever was coming. She slipped through her room window and snuck off the Shifter compound and headed to The Resistance hang out that had been attacked by Vampires. Enora would have been called to tend to the wounded. Despite her work with the dead, it seemed she was also the de facto trauma doctor for the Aura as well.

.....

Keeping a watchful eye on Jaq, Enora did her best to focus on the task at hand. Stitching the wounded and making arrangements for the unlucky ones to be transported to the morgue. The Aura and human casualties, at least. The Shifters would handle their own. And the Vampires? Well, they would have to handle their dead on their own. Enora was done covering for them. Especially, after tonight.

Deep down, she knew not all Vampires were monsters like those who had attacked The Resistance hang out, but that didn't excuse those that were. Speaking of monsters, she couldn't get the visual of Jaq bloodied and full of rage stalking toward her out of her head. His eyes had burned into her soul as his fingers dug into the flesh around her arm. He hadn't meant to hurt her, but her skin still smarted where he'd grabbed her. He was upset, she rationalized, but she also didn't like that side of Jaq. Before today, she knew he was powerful but had never seen him as the violent type. Now, she knew otherwise. Something else to add to the list of reasons continuing on with him was not an option.

"I think we're all done here," she said to Mack who was helping her guide the survivors through examinations and debriefing before sending them home.

Mack nodded after sending the last group on their way. Donovan and Hendrex huddled with Jaq and Tyr Greywulf, the leader of the Langsmith Shifter pack. The Vampires who helped at the monster house raid were talking to the Vampire Jaq had stopped from killing an Aura boy. Enora was tempted to eavesdrop on their conversations, but exhaustion swept over her. Today had been the longest day of her life, between Ruling One's death, finding out she carried Jaq's child, and now, this blatant attack by the Vampires. Enora just wanted to go home, to lock herself in the safety of her home and not emerge until all the death and destruction were done with.

"You look tired, maybe you should crash with me and Rye tonight," Mack offered.

Enora sighed. The offer was tempting, but staying with them meant more questions from Disrayan about who her baby daddy was. She wasn't sure she could stand Disrayan's penetrating gaze in the state she was in. She forced a smile and shook her head.

"Thanks for the offer, but I'll be fine."

Mack eyed her and opened his mouth to say something but was interrupted by the Vampires calling him over.

"Don't leave yet, I'll at least make sure you get home okay," he said before taking off toward the others.

Enora didn't wait for him. Instead, she packed her things and headed to her car. On the way, she pulled out her phone and opened the group text for Farrah, Disrayan, and Zazzie.

E: Vampires killed Ruling One and then attacked The Resistance clubhouse. Be safe ladies.

She wasn't sure how in the loop her friends were with everything. Enora didn't exactly trust the men to share all the details with them either. All three responded almost immediately.

Z: Oh no!

D: Damn.

F: Fuck all!

E: Right?

D: I'm guessing that's where Mack ran off to.

E: Yep all the men were there.

F: Assholes, trying to keep us out of the loop.

Z: Lol, I am glad to be safely at home. Thanks.

D: Are you okay, E?

F: Also, who's the baby daddy?

E: On my way home now.

She didn't bother replying to Farrah. They would know when she was ready to tell them and not a moment sooner. Hell, she was still wrapping her head around the whole thing. She started her car only to jump when Jaq slid into the passenger seat.

"Get out," she said, but he ignored her and buckled his seatbelt.

"I'm just making sure you get home okay. We need to talk, but now isn't the right time for either of us," he said.

Enora bit her lip and shook her head.

"You can't keep forcing yourself into my life like this." He took her hand in his and brought it to his lips.

"Let's get you home, love. No important talks right now."

With a sigh, she pulled away from the curb. She was too tired to fight with him, especially when it would delay her getting home and getting into bed.

.....

The last thing Jaq wanted to do was leave Enora's side. He wanted to walk through the front door with her. Run her a relaxing bath and massage away the tension in her body. He wanted to pamper her and pleasure her until the horrors of the night were an afterthought. Instead, he walked her to her door and gave her kiss before allowing her to slip away.

"Lock the doors, okay?" he said. She flicked him off before slamming the door in his face.

He waited until he heard the dead bolt slide into place before he backed off her porch. He wanted to stay, but he couldn't. He had a mission of his own that night. The Vampires who'd attacked eventually spilled the beans on who was behind it and where to find him.

For all Jaq knew, it was a trap, but he was willing to take the risk. He wasn't going to let the attack against his people go unanswered.

Jasper waited for him down the block from Enora's. He hopped into the truck and was immediately handed a weapon which he waved away.

"Guns aren't my thing," he said, earning him a smirk and a nod of understanding.

"I'm just glad you are finally seeing things my way," Jasper said.

Jaq rolled his eyes. He still didn't agree with Jasper's way of things. This was different. He wasn't attacking first; this was a pre-emptive strike. The Vampires thought they were weak, but after tonight, Jaq would show them that they had messed with the wrong Aura.

Jaq guided Jasper to the address the Vampire had given. Xander, Claude, and Greg were already there waiting, along with a petite blonde.

"Who is this?" Jaq asked.

The blonde smiled, revealing a set of sharp fangs, and approached him.

"Hi, I'm Carrie, and the house you want entrance to belongs to my father," she said.

Jaq tensed and so did the members of The Resistance that had come along, but Greg stepped forward as if to guard the woman.

"She's here to help. Maximus attacked me and Mack earlier to get to her. She's our way in the front door," he explained.

"I plan to kill your father. You okay with that?" Jaq asked, knowing the answer by her sharp intake of breath.

She whirled on Greg.

"You said nothing about killing him," she snapped.

Greg glared at Jaq, but he just shrugged it off. He wasn't about to go in there and risk her turning against him when it came to the final moments.

"We won't be killing Maximus, just sending him a clear message that his actions won't be tolerated," Xander said stepping forward.

"I vote we kill him," another female voice said from behind

them.

Jaq turned to see the owner of Club Obelisk, Molly, dressed in all black and armed with an impressive looking sword. Behind her stood two other armed Vampire females and a Vampire male who Jaq recognized as Shane.

"Really, Shane, you had one job," Claude said. Shane shrugged.

"You really thought you could continue to sneak off after Maura was handled and they not notice?"

Jaq shook his head.

"Look, I don't care what you all have planned, but I'm going in there and wrecking some shit, end of story."

He signaled for the members of The Resistance to follow him and used his energy to open a hole in the perimeter fence. Those on board with his plan followed. The only people not to cross through were Greg and Carrie.

"Leave them. Stupid bitch won't be of any help," Molly said, and Shane sighed.

"Molly, Carrie is..." She raised her hand and stopped him mid-sentence.

"The woman who stalked you from rehab? The one whose father is a slave-holding, egoist asshat? Yeah, let Greg keep her over there while we put an end to this bloodsucking fiend," she snapped.

Jaq smiled; he was suddenly a major fan of this woman.

"Seriously, Molly. Let's get this over with so we can go home and finally have a life without a target on our backs," the Vivica Fox lookalike Vampire said and marched toward the mansion sword in hand.

Xander strode confidently after her, while Claude stuck close to the mousy one with the scarf tied around her neck. Jaq was surprised by the pairings of mates. No wonder the men stayed in their own mansion most of the time. Who could blame them with hot pieces like those? Jaq had a hot piece of his own to get back to, so he quickly released the energy holding the fence open and prepared for the next stage. Breaching the mansion.

Head Knocker

Ruling Three rolled over on the overly soft mattress and groaned. His head was killing him, his limbs felt heavy and weak. At least, he was still alive. That was more than he could say for Ruling One. Maximus had forced him to watch as he drained Ruling One of blood completely. Her body had paled and gone limp, then shriveled like a raisin in the sun when Maximus allowed his men to drain the last drops from her body.

A dried husk was all that was left when they were done, and then they'd gone after him. He groaned, remembering the fiery agony that ran through him as multiple pairs of fangs pierced his flesh. He shuddered and tried to move, but there was a tugging at his wrists.

Looking down, he saw that he was bound to the bed by both wrists and a needle was stuck at the crook of each arm. Long thin tubes ran from his body, crimson with his blood. They were still draining him but slowly this time.

"Oh! You're awake," a soft feminine voice said.

Ruling Three couldn't see who was talking, they were out of his line of sight. A second later, she came into view, like an angel of mercy she held a straw to his lips. He sipped the cool, sweet liquid she offered.

"This will help," she said.

"Who are you?"

She smiled and shook her head.

"It doesn't matter. I will only be here a short while. Master has you now, and I have betrayed him," she said.

Ruling Three frowned.

"Master? Betrayed?"

"Shhh, rest now."

He felt a calming energy overwhelm him, but he was too weak to fight it with his own. His eyelids grew heavy and began to drift closed. He was almost out again when there was a loud bang above, followed by the sound of rushing feet.

"Help," he mouthed but no sound came from his throat. It was too late. Whatever happened upstairs, he wouldn't be of witness to as the darkness overcame him.

.....

Surging forward, Jaq knocked three Vampires out of his way. Like bowling pins, they fell around him before his guys fired on them. Jaq didn't care whether Maximus's henchmen lived or died. All that mattered was cutting off the head of the snake.

He pushed into the room in which he'd seen Molly disappear. She'd managed to walk right passed all the guards without taking a single swipe with her sword. They fell to their knees, toppling like dominoes before crumbling into ash in her wake. Jaq had never seen power like that in his life. No wonder Maximus had been afraid of her.

The others were in various stages of battle from the foyer to the hall. Shots rang out, blades clanged, even the thrumming whack of a bow and arrow mingled with the grunts and screams of landed blows and physical exertion. The death toll here would surely be greater than the Vampires initial attack on The Resistance.

Jaq stepped over several such dead bodies before entering the room. The battle noise was muffled by the rows of bookcases surrounding the grand desk at the center of the room. Molly stood behind the desk holding Maximus by his throat.

"Where is the girl?" she demanded.

Maximus flicked a glance in Jaq's direction before smirking.

"If you kill me, neither of you will get what you want," he hissed.

Jaq rolled his eyes and moved closer.

"Here, let me," he said.

Molly looked as if she would rather snap Maximus's neck before letting him go. She pouted before setting him back in the chair, her blade firmly against his neck.

Jaq moved closer and placed his hands-on Maximus's temples. Donovan Mars wasn't the only one who could get into people's heads. Jaq was unprepared for how hard it was to actually see into Maximus's mind. Years of drinking Aura blood had helped him build a tolerance to Aura energy. As if sensing Jaq's struggle, Molly pressed the blade farther into Maximus's neck.

"Maybe I'll slit your precious daughter's throat once I'm done with you. She may be more forthcoming than Daddy Dearest," she sneered.

"You wouldn't dare," Maximus growled, but his anger was enough for Jaq to latch onto a ride past his protections.

What Jaq saw made his skin crawl. Countless Aura women, so much hatred. Power and madness, deceit and assassinations. Maximus was not only a threat to the Aura, but to his own kind. Jaq and Molly would be doing the world a favor by ridding it of this madman. Jaq pulled his energy from the Vampire's thoughts. Like thick sludge, his darkness clung to Jaq, making him feel ill. Jaq stumbled back, and Molly grabbed his arm to help steady him.

Her quick reaction gave Maximus the opening he needed to try to get away. He slid from the chair and raced toward the door, but Molly was no ordinary Vampire, and she sure as hell wasn't an ordinary Aura. A blinding white light emanated from her body, like overexposure on a camera. Jaq could see nothing except her. Hear nothing but the death knells of Maximus by the door. Then, as quick as it started, Molly crumpled to the floor, the light gone except for crackling sparks around her fingertips.

"Maximus was nothing but a pile of dust by the door.

"Damn," was all Jaq could say before he knelt to check on Molly. She was still breathing, but the amount of energy she'd used had knocked her unconscious.

Save her…

Molly's voice rang inside Jaq's head.

He stumbled back, unsure if he had overtaxed himself to the point of hallucinating. He heard it again.

Save her. Save them all.

With a nod, Jaq backed out of the office, closing the door behind him. The others were still picking off who was left in Maximus's guard. He followed his knowledge from Maximus into the basement holding cells. His energy was tapped out, and the Vampires kept there looked prime for a fight. It was too late to go back and get help; they'd seen him and would easily overtake him with their Vampire speed. He took a deep breath and squared his shoulders before charging at the bigger one. If he got enough momentum, maybe he could knock them both over and the big one would crush the smaller one.

His plan only half worked. The big one dodged him and pushed him toward the smaller one whose fist connected with Jaq's stomach. Jaq, unable to right himself, kicked backwards and caught the bigger Vampire in the knee cap while he rammed his head into the stomach of the smaller one. The bigger Vampire fell to one knee as Jaq pushed the other against the wall and wailed on him with everything he had.

The smaller Vampire took the punches like they were nothing and brought his elbow across Jaq's back. Jaq crumpled to the floor, his vision clearing enough for him to see the foot coming toward his face in enough time to roll out of the way. Only for the big Vampire to catch him in the gut again from the other side.

"Go easy on him, Butch. Maybe we can get a meal out of this one before we kill him," the smaller Vampire said.

Butch grinned and yanked Jaq from the ground.

"Always knew you were a smart one," Butch laughed.

His putrid breath stung Jaq's nose before the man reared back, fangs elongating, ready to strike, and then his body jerked and his eyes went wide.

Jaq slid from the man's grip and hit the ground again. He saw a projectile whiz by and strike the smaller Vampire through the heart. A second later, the mousy brunette stood over him with a toothy grin.

"Hi! I'm Gretchen, in case you want to know who just saved your life," she said and helped him to his feet.

"Thanks," he managed.

"Those two were the last ones, I think," she said brightly.

Jaq shook his head.

"Maximus has people imprisoned here; we need to help them."

The smile on her face faltered, and she turned toward the door the guards had been blocking. She readied another arrow while Jaq crept forward and opened the door. There was no one visible on the other side. Just a set of stairs with another short hall at the bottom.

"I'll go first," Jaq said, but Gretchen rolled her eyes before using her Vampire speed to go ahead without him.

He rushed down the stairs after her, finding her already moving through the hall and checking each door like a pro.

"Do all you Vampires get tactical training?" he asked.

She held up her fingers to shush him before kicking in one of the doors with her bow ready to fire at anything that came at her. When she didn't immediately fire, Jaq moved into the room. There was only one person there, and Jaq couldn't care less about saving him.

Ruling Three was laid on a bed with blood being drawn from both arms. If anyone else had found him, they would assume he was just another victim, but the others hadn't seen inside Maximus's head like he had. Jaq walked to the bed and snatched the pillow out from under Ruling Three's head before pressing it over his face.

"What are you doing?" Gretchen said, rushing forward to stop him.

"Bastard sold out his own people," Jaq growled.

There was movement out of the corner of his eye before Gretchen turned away from him and grabbed the arms of the woman who had been about to hit him with a vase.

"What the hell?"

Claude came storming into the room, followed by a few of The Resistance members. Jaq scowled and tossed the pillow to the side.

If he killed Ruling Three now, he would look like the bad guy.

"Grab Ruling Three and the chick, and let's get the fuck out of here," Jaq barked and stormed out of the room.

.....

Enora tried her best to get some rest but her brain just wouldn't shut off. She stared at her white stucco ceilings and imagined white fluffy sheep bounding overhead. The problem was as they reached the ground their heads fell off and their wool matted with blood. She glanced at her clock for the fifth time that night. It was one am. Just five more hours for her to try to get some sleep.

When her brain wasn't decapitating sheep, it was remembering the horror scenes from the monster house or The Resistance clubhouse. If not those, it was about Jaq and what he might be doing at that very moment. Was he drinking himself into oblivion with Mack, or bedding some tramp he picked up at Obelisk? He surely hadn't stuck around to be with her, to comfort her.

With a groan, she tossed back the sheets and got out of bed. If she wasn't going to sleep, she would just have a cup of tea and read. Maybe a few chapters would distract her brain enough to allow her to sleep. She grabbed her phone and crept down the stairs to her kitchen. The shadows along the stairs made her uneasy.

Maybe she should have taken Mack up on the offer to stay with him and Disrayan. It wasn't so long ago that Disrayan had been kidnapped by Vampires. They were obviously being bolder about their attacks. Disrayan was the Magistrate, Ruling One was part of the Ruling Council. They were targeting the most powerful of them.

She turned on her kitchen light, the warm glow of the yellow Edison bulbs bringing some warmth to the room and her thoughts. She filled her tea kettle and set it on the stove before grabbing her throw blanket and curling into her favorite chair to read. She was only halfway into the first chapter when her eyes began to droop. She yawned and snuggled tighter into her blanket, pretending that its warmth wasn't just her own cocooned inside the fiber, but that of Jaq wrapping his muscled arms around her waist and spooning her body.

She began to nod off only to awaken to the shrill scream of her tea pot. Maybe tea had been a bad idea after all. She jumped up to move it from the stove, dropping her phone in the process. She was wide awake again, so she poured herself a cup and went back to her chair. She picked up her phone and glanced at it for the first time since she arrived home.

She frowned when she saw a fairly long thread on the Aura Underground. It was the gossip site started by a couple of Aura on the outside, something like a neighborhood watch meets community gossip site. She was only subscribed because it was a good way to find the families of unidentified Aura who came into the morgue.

"Fucking hell," she cursed before abandoning her tea to run to her room and get dressed. Word had gotten out about Ruling One and the attack on The Resistance. Added with Disrayan's kidnapping, and the Aura outside of Ceres were panicking. Several families had expressed their desire to return to Ceres, but with gate crossings being restricted again, that required several layers of red tape that some weren't willing to wait for.

As she read further, she saw those who planned to storm the gate. That was a bad idea when the gate was under normal operations. At this point, people would die trying to make it across without proper medical care. She hoped she could get there in time to stop as many as she could, but she would need help.

E: 911 Gate Now!

With the text sent, she called each of her girls individually to make sure they got the message.

Farrah and Donovan lived the closest to the gate, so she arrived first, followed by Disrayan and Mack, then Zazzie and Hendrex. The gate had been opened, and the three couples stood in front of it, blocking people from entering as best they could.

"It's not safe to cross," Hendrex shouted.

"Why should we believe you?" "You told us it was safer here!" "Move out of the way!"

The crowd shouted back. It was madness and chaos as people pushed and shoved their way forward. Enora couldn't even reach her friends to help. She could only stand and watch in horror as they were overtaken and people rushed the gate. They were helpless to stop those most desperate without making the situation worse. They relented and moved to the side, shaking their heads as Aura fled the human world back to Ceres.

"I should make sure they are alright," Enora said when the last of the crowd either changed their mind and left or crossed into Ceres.

Zazzie grabbed her arm and shook her head.

"Not in your condition, it's too dangerous," she hissed low enough for only Enora to hear.

She wanted to protest but thought better of it. Enora wasn't sure what she was going to do about the baby yet, but it wasn't right for her to endanger the child's life without Jaq knowing anything about it. Speaking of Jaq, everyone was there except for him. Maybe no one had called him, but it still didn't sit right with her that he had been nowhere around to try to convince the scared crowd that the human world was where they should stay.

In fact, none of The Resistance members were present. That didn't jive with their whole mission. Someone should have been here.

"Where's Jaq? Where is The Resistance in all of this?"

Everyone looked at each other with equal amounts of question and confusion.

"Damn idiot," Mack cursed.

"What?"

"The Resistance isn't here because they are going after the Vampires," Donovan said.

"They're what?" Farrah pulled out her phone and dialed who Enora could only assume was Jaq.

Relief flooded through Enora when Jaq apparently answered and Farrah tore into him.

"You stupid, idiotic, reckless...." Farrah paused in her tirade to listen to something Jaq had to say.

She lowered her phone and put it on speaker. Enora's heart skipped a beat when Jaq's voice rang out into the night.

"We killed Maximus and rescued an Aura woman from his basement. Ruling Three is also in our custody," Jaq said.

"You don't have a custody," Donovan snapped.

"You're still stupid, do you realize what's going to happen once the Vampires find out you killed one of their own?" Mack sighed.

"They'll fucking thank me for it. Asshole had plans to assassinate his own kind for power," Jaq said.

"Your ass is lucky to be alive," Hendrex chimed in.

"Farrah, take me off speaker and give Enora the phone," Jaq said.

Farrah's eyes went wide as she stared between the phone and Enora's stomach.

"Oh, fuck no," she cursed and hung up the phone.

"Farrah," Zazzie warned, coming to Enora's defense.

"Look, I'm not angry, well, I didn't put the obvious clues together."

Farrah rambled while the men remained perplexed about what was going on. Enora felt her phone buzzing in her pocket, but she refused to answer it at the moment.

"The way you are reacting is exactly why she didn't mention it before," Disrayan said.

"How would you react to finding out one of your best friends is secretly dating your brother?"

"Farrah!" Zazzie scolded her.

"Wait, you're Jaq's girlfriend?"

"Damn straight, she is."

Enora froze at the sound of Jaq's voice. Instantly grateful Farrah had the presence of mind not to share the fact that she was also probably pregnant by Jaq. That was something she just did not want to deal with on top of everything else. Everyone stared at her and Enora put her face in her hands and shook her head.

"I might be," she said lamely.

Jaq closed the distance between them and pulled her into his arms.

"You are," he stated, and the pride and hope shining in his eyes was her undoing.

"We haven't really discussed labels."

"Does it have to be a discussion?"

"I wanted to be sure before anyone else found out, but right now is not the time to discuss this. What the hell is your problem? Why would you attack the Vampires?"

He tensed and pulled away.

"You expected me to not retaliate?"

"Well no, but to pull a stunt like this without back up, without considering the options."

He shook his head.

"Maximus wasn't going to stop. He was the mastermind behind the blood slave trade, not the rogues. He planned to overthrow the Vampire Council once he was strong enough from Aura blood. Getting rid of him was necessary, and couldn't wait for him to gear up and plan for us coming for him."

"What about Ruling Three and the girl? Where are they?" Donovan asked.

"The woman is safe at a refugee shelter, and Ruling three is in the car. I plan to toss his ass off a mountain after he confesses to someone other than me what he's done."

"And what has he done?" Disrayan asked.

"Donovan," Jaq said, making a sweeping motion to where his truck was parked.

Donovan strode over and opened the door. Ruling Three laid across the backseat, hands and legs bound.

"Don't you dare touch me!" he screeched.

Donovan didn't listen, placing his hands on either side of Ruling Three's brain. He tensed, sweat breaking out on his forehead, brow furrowed until he pulled away with a growl.

"Murderer!"

"Exactly," Jaq said and shut the truck door.

"He must stand trial. If anything happens to him by our hand it will only make us look bad," Hendrex stepped forward.

"Stand trial? By who? You know damn well if we hand him over now, he will get elected and nothing will happen to him," Mack said.

"Have faith in the Aura," Hendrex said.

"Like you did? Look where that got ya, bud," Jaq said.

"No one knows he is missing yet. Maybe we do drop him off a mountain and no one has to know," Disrayan chimed in.

Everyone stared at her, that was the last thing any of them expected her to say.

"As much as I would love to rid the Aura of this traitorous bastard, we need to do this right. I will escort him back to Ceres myself," Donovan said.

Fall

Jaq didn't like the idea of letting Ruling Three go back to Ceres, but in his weakened state, there was always a chance he would die in the treacherous crossing. He allowed Donovan and Hendrex to pull Ruling Three out of the car and carry him to the gate. The others followed, but Jaq grabbed Enora's arm to stop her.

"You can't go, it's too dangerous," he said, and for a moment, he thought she might protest but then her shoulders slumped.

"I guess someone has to be here to clean up this mess," she grumbled and stalked off toward her car.

Jaq signaled for Jasper to follow the others through the gate. Enora wasn't acting herself, and he didn't want to leave her before he had an idea of why.

"Make sure they don't screw this up," he said to Jasper before chasing after Enora.

She said nothing as he pulled her into his arms.

"You want to talk about it?"

She kept her eyes straight ahead, everywhere but on him.

"Now isn't the time," she said after a moment.

He sighed. So, this was about them.

"When will it be the right time? After the elections? When Ceres falls?"

She looked at him, steel behind the sadness in her eyes.

"I don't want to talk about this."

"Fine, no talking." He reached out to touch her cheek.

She turned into his touch, pressing a kiss on his palm, and a single tear rolled down her cheek. He knew he wasn't going to like what she had to say next.

"I can't do this anymore, Jaq. There is no us, there never should have been."

She turned away from him but didn't leave. His heart screamed for him to get on one knee, to make her see that they were meant to be. To show her what they had wasn't just physical, but his ego wouldn't let him. Not in front of members of The Resistance who watched from a few feet away. He had to show strength in front of them. No signs of weakness in this tumultuous time. He was their leader before all else. Including, the love of his life, at least right now. Defeated, he puffed up his chest and rolled his eyes.

"I don't have time for these games, Enora. Let me know when you stop lying to yourself. I've got more important things to do than beg your ass," he spat.

She shot daggers at him with her eyes before storming to her car. He felt every one of them in his heart, but he schooled his face not to let it show. He could hear her grumbling about immature assholes as she left him, but that only fueled his pain and anger. He forced himself to turn away and marched toward the gate.

"It's time The Resistance made their presence known in Ceres," he barked and drew the necessary runes on the wall.

It took several minutes for the runes to spread and create the opening to Ceres. The Aura in the group each grabbed the arm of a non-Aura to help them through. Jaq was breaking all the rules tonight. Why not? His heart had been shattered into a million pieces, why not share. They tried to cross, but the first non-Aura to try received a jolt of energy so strong it knocked him on his ass. Even in its weakened state, the protections were still in place, and Jaq could do nothing about it from the outside.

"You stay with him until he wakes. The rest of us will go ahead," he ordered.

The non-Aura weren't happy about being left behind, but Jaq was sure they would rather not be electrocuted either. He didn't wait for the grumbling to start. Instead, he stepped through, tensing in preparation for the physical onslaught traveling through the gate caused.

What Jaq wasn't prepared for was the sight of Ceres when he finally crossed. The artificial wind whipped furiously through the gardens, dust and leaves obscuring even more than the dense fog. He could almost taste the Ozone; the air was so thick. He pushed his way forward, only managing to stay on the path from memory as the amount of visible light left in the sky was practically nil.

When he reached the outer ring of Magelor, the wind was calmer, but the streets were darker and full of potential hazards. Merchants' wares littered the cobbled pathway, and despite feeling the presence of others as he got closer to the Meeting House, Jaq had the eerie feeling of being utterly alone. Someone with his reputation would be avoided during controversial times such as these. For all he knew, they blamed him for the trouble Ceres was in. The Ruling Council wasn't exactly known for taking the credit for anything bad that happened to their people. Not a soul was seen until he finally reached the Meeting House. Pulling the door open, he pushed inside, joining what appeared to be everyone left in Ceres as they filed into the Meeting Room.

.....

Enora sat in her car. She should just drive away. Go home and try to sleep before her shift at the morgue. Yet, even though she was able to start the car, she couldn't make herself leave. She told herself it was because all of her friends had crossed into Ceres, but she knew it was because she wanted to make sure Jaq and his crew crossed over safely.

Sure, he'd been an ass to her, but she had started it. She might not want to be with him, but that didn't stop her from caring. After idling for what seemed like forever, Enora cursed and stopped the engine before getting out of the car. Elections were supposed to happen today anyway, if they weren't postponed because of the evidence against Ruling Three.

She would go to Ceres, or at the very least help others cross safely. When she rounded the corner of the factory, she gasped and took off at a run. Three people lay unconscious on the ground.

"What the hell happened?" she demanded of the crowd.

They stared at her before anyone answered.

"They tried to cross."

Enora shook her head.

"Idiots," she cursed and pulled out her keys to the factory. "There are medical supplies stored just inside the door. Get them now!"

The man didn't hesitate before taking the keys and running off to do her bidding. Enora checked her three new patients.

"How long have they been down?" she asked as she checked for a pulse and to make sure they were still breathing.

"Just a few minutes. The gate shocked them, and they just passed out," another one answered.

Thankfully, after a quick examination, she didn't think they were in any immediate danger. Still, as two of them were human and the third a Shifter, she didn't want to risk anyone dying right in front of the gate.

She pulled out her phone and dialed the human authorities before instructing the other humans in the group to move them out of the alley. As for the Shifter, she dialed her contact in the local pack and had the other Shifters move away from the gate as well. The Shifters should heal faster than the humans, but they should all pull through okay. She hoped.

There was a reason Enora chose to work in the morgue, beside it being a place to intercept Aura bodies to be interred properly. She couldn't stand the thought of anyone dying by her hands. She never wanted anyone's life to depend on her. Her thoughts jumped to her possible pregnancy. If she had this baby, this life would be hers to care for. Hers to protect from the madness and hatred in the world. A world where they would be immediately judged by the color of their skin, a world where their gender would determine if they were a ball-buster or a go-getter. A world where they could never truly be themselves outside of small intimate circles of friends and family.

Enora tried to stand, but her legs were too wobbly. She leaned against the brick wall next to the gate as her heart raced in her chest and her stomach twisted in knots. She gulped in air, desperate to fill her lungs and stave off the panic creeping through her body, paralyzing her with fear. Fear of the moment, fear for the future. Her vision began to blur, and she pulled on all of her strength to stay conscious long enough to call for help. Her voice was barely above her normal speaking voice as she tried to scream, but it would be enough for any Shifter, or Horus forbid, Vampire nearby to hear.

.....

Sarah ran over as soon as she saw Jaq's mate crumple against the wall. Sarah should have been back at the Shifter compound, but hadn't been able to resist coming back to town to watch the gate. Tyr would be upset with her when he found out she had snuck off, especially after the attack on The Resistance. He and Sequoia had gone full parental mode and tried to keep her in the cabin all night.

Sarah was too much of a free spirit to spend that much time indoors. It didn't feel natural to her, so here she was. Holding Jaq's girlfriend in her arms and trying to wake her. The Aura was still breathing, and her heartbeat had slowed back to normal for the most part, but her eyes just wouldn't open. It was like her soul was hiding.

She could relate to that. Sarah helped her into a sitting position and used her Shifter heat to help keep Enora warm until Jaq and the others crossed back to the human world. Sarah had come here for answers, and now she had them. Even with the help of an Aura, it was impossible for anyone else to cross into Ceres. A small piece of the hope she'd held onto for a safe haven died at the realization, but she had to remind herself that the information she had gathered from the Aura in The Resistance told her that even the Great Sanctuary wasn't the utopia she and others had always dreamed it was.

A soft breeze blew through the loading zone, carrying with it the scent of fresh blood before her ears picked up the rumble of a running crowd. She pulled herself away from Enora and prepared for a fight. In a matter of minutes, a stampede of Aura rounded the corner, a group of Vampires on their heels. Sarah's senses were overwhelmed, and she knew there was little she could do against the sheer number of panicked Aura or the blood craved Vamps at their backs. She turned back to Enora, who as still slumbering against the wall, and cursed.

"I can't just leave you here," she muttered and pulled Enora from the ground.

Tossing her over her shoulders, Sarah used every bit of her strength to carry her away from the gate to Ceres. The frightened Aura were too panicked to bother with her, and the Vampires were honed in on the Aura who were already bleeding. It was just enough of a distraction for her to get Enora around the corner and mostly out of harm's way.

None of the Aura or The Resistance safehouses she was aware of would be safe at this point. The Vampires were on the attack for a very specific prey. That meant Sarah had to get Enora to the Shifter safehouse which would be a whole other issue for her to deal with later. She didn't have time to contemplate all the consequences of her actions. She just knew she needed to get both of them out of there and quick.

.....

In the center of the Meeting Room, Donovan and Hendrex stood next to Ruling Three who was propped up in a chair that had been brought in just for him. Commander Mars stood on one side of the inner circle preparing the ceremonial box in which all voting took place in Ceres. Ruling Two stood on the other side of the room, forcing a smile and attempting to make pleasantries with those who would listen.

Jaq shook his head and pushed his way through the crowd. They couldn't possibly be thinking about doing elections right now, in the middle of Ceres crashing around them and with no mention of Ruling Three's treachery and Ruling One's untimely demise. He didn't stop, even as a Security Force Officer grabbed his arm to keep him out of the inner circle. He shrugged the man off and stormed to where Ruling Three sat and slapped him across the face. The crisp snap of his hand contacting Ruling Three's cheek stunned everyone to silence, all eyes turned on him.

"Wake up, you prick, and tell them what you did," Jaq demanded.

He knew the man was awake, his breathing wasn't as shallow as before, and the man had scowled after being slapped across the face. Ruling Three continued to let his head loll forward as if he were unresponsive, and Jaq raised his hand to slap him again but Hendrex grabbed his arm.

"Cousin, I think that's enough," he said.

Jaq glared at him until he saw the twinkle of amusement in Hendrex's eyes. At least, he wasn't trying to defend the bastard, but rather trying to help Jaq stay out of Security Force custody. He registered the Officers moving closer in his peripheral. Donovan stepped in their way, and they backed off.

Jaq sighed and turned to face the crowd he'd just pushed through.

"Voting now is a mistake. You don't have all the facts. Not all the Aura are present," he tried to reason with the crowd.

"Says the traitor!" someone shouted.

Jaq rolled his eyes.

"The only traitor in this room is feigning sleep like a coward. He has been working with the Vampires, he killed Ruling One, he arranged for the kidnapping of the Magistrate, which led to her being removed from the trial against my cousin. Ruling Three is the biggest traitor there ever was in the history of Ceres," Jaq said.

"Lies!" Ruling Three practically jumped from his seat.

Donovan grabbed the man by the shoulders and pushed him back onto the chair.

"What a miraculous recovery," he sneered.

"The gods granted me a respite to defend my honor," Ruling Three replied.

"The gods have nothing to do with your delusions," Hendrex said.

"Enough of this! We need to establish new leadership. It is obvious that without it we are no better than the humans," Ruling Two spoke.

There was a murmur through the crowd as if they were unsure

if they wanted to vote now or continue to watch the soap opera unfolding before them. Eventually, they died down and a man stepped forward.

"We vote," he announced, and the Security Force Officers began handing out the parchment and charcoal used as ballots in Ceres.

The sheets were completely blank. There was no need to list names when the options were so limited. Jaq accepted a sheet of paper from one of the Officers, ignoring the disapproving stare of those who believed him to be a traitor. The same faces that had looked down on him before he left Ceres. Those who had called him a nuisance and a troublemaker. They had no idea then how much their disdain had grown on him, had spurred him to become the man he was. They wanted a troublemaker, they got one, just not in the way they imagined.

Jaq cut a glance back at Ruling Three before scribbling Donovan's name on the paper. Jaq may not have agreed with the previous Council Members, but this was a chance for real change. While they weren't completely on the same page, Jaq knew in his heart that Donovan not only had the best interest of the Aura at heart, but he wasn't opposed to breaking tradition to get things done. Not to mention, the guy probably would hate being restricted in his duties if elected. That was petty enough for Jaq in that moment. He also added Disrayan, Mack, and lastly, for lack of a better option, himself.

As people made their choices, they cycled through to place their ballots in the box. Jaq folded his paper and got in line with the rest of them. These things usually went pretty quickly, but this time it seemed people were unsure of what to do. They wanted to do the vote early, but obviously hadn't considered the consequences of doing so without an established candidate field.

Not to mention, they were missing too many people for the elections to be called right then and there. Jaq dropped his vote into the box when there was a loud boom, a flood of energy, swept over him like the surge in Langsmith. He was able to stay conscious, but it still knocked him to his knees.

He was one of the lucky ones. Several other Aura had fallen, and from the look on people's faces, there were some who were no longer amongst the living. Ruling Three was the first to push to his feet.

"This is a sign! We must fight for the survival of Ceres," he called.

Jaq shook his head, figures the man would make a play for power in the middle of a disaster. Jaq stood and brushed the dirt from his knees.

"More like a sign that we shouldn't be doing this now. The Aura deserve the right to make an informed vote."

"The Aura know who they want to lead. Don't try to confuse the matter for your own gain," Ruling Three snarled.

"Says the man who destabilized the Barrier to boost his own energy," Jaq snapped.

The Meeting Room was silent except for them. Donovan and Hendrex helped those who were injured out of the room. Commander Mars stood guard by the voting box while the few Security Force officers, still with their faculties intact, gathered those who had fallen. Jaq faced off with Ruling Three. Energy crackled in the air between them.

"Baseless accusations from the traitor," Ruling Three said.

"Enough of this," Commander Mars barked. "With the interest of the safety of our people in mind, I postpone the vote until a more appropriate time."

Ruling Three whirled on Commander Mars.

"Are you agreeing with the traitor?"

Commander Mars glared at Ruling Three.

"I am acting in the best interest of the Aura. Half our population isn't present, and a quarter of those here have been incapacitated by an unknown surge of energy. My duty is to protect the people and the sanctuary of Ceres. I cannot do my job if I am stuck babysitting you two bickering brats," Commander Mars said.

He lifted the voting box and placed it back on its secure shelf before storming from the room, barking orders at his men to facilitate clean up and figure out where the surge of energy came from. Ruling Three squared his shoulders and faced the remaining crowd.

"I have been chosen by the gods. It is my right, my duty, to lead and protect you all. As evidence of my divine right, I will show you who holds the key to ensuring the continued safety and prosperity of our people," he said and marched out of the Meeting Room.

A gaggle of people followed, and dread settled in Jaq's stomach like a lead weight. He forced himself to follow as well.

Ruling Three lead them up the stairs to the Balancing Crystal. The officers left to guard the crystal were on the ground, ashen and unmoving. The crystal itself glowed a dull red. Ruling Three stretched out his hand's palms toward the crystal, he began to chant. The red glow intensified and began to return to the purple hue synonymous with the Ceresian sky. His followers looked on in awe as it appeared that he was fixing the Barrier all on his own. Jaq knew better. He could feel the crystal pulling on not only Ruling Three but everyone in the room. Could feel that nothing about the purple hue was normal.

"We need to go," he said, but no one was listening.

Like moths to a flame, they joined Ruling Three in his chanting. Sacrificing their energy in a vain attempt to stabilize the Barrier. As their energy waned, the red hue crept back in, the temperature in the room crept up several degrees. Everything in Jaq screamed for him to run. The crystal began to hum an unnatural low tone. One by one, the weaker of Ruling Three's followers began to fall.

Jaq grabbed the woman closest to him. The last survivor besides Ruling Three. She screamed and kicked as he dragged her away from the crystal. Away from certain death. He rushed down the stairs, the crystal still pulling at him, at his energy, but the farther he managed to get, the less the pull. He ran to the Security Force Office and kicked in the door.

"We need to evacuate now!"

His cries fell on deaf ears once again. Shaking his head, Jaq did the one thing he swore he would never do. He let his energy flow, no barriers, no holds. He infiltrated the minds of all those within his reach and showed them what he had seen. From Maximus, to Ruling Three, to the crystal dropping Aura like flies. He knew he couldn't keep this up for long, and he also wasn't too keen on dying in Ceres. Keeping his connection open, he forced his body to move, half of his brain concentrated on broadcasting the truth, the other on pushing himself back toward the gate.

He needed to get there before there wasn't enough energy left for him to cross safely. If he was going to die, he wanted to die in the arms of the woman he loved. To see her face one last time, to apologize for what he said earlier, and if he was lucky, kiss her one last time.

Run

"Jaq," Enora woke to his name on her lips. Something was wrong, seriously wrong. It took a moment for her brain to catch up. She was being carried by someone. Someone not Jaq.

"Shhh, we need to get out of here," a female voice said.

Enora stiffened as fear flooded her body. The woman groaned and nearly dropped her on the ground. Enora was able to get her feet down first and save them both the trouble.

"What happened?" Enora asked.

The girl flipped her brown hair out of her face. Enora instantly recognized her as the Shifter teen from The Resistance.

"The Vampires are attacking the Aura. They are slaughtering them at the gate. I need to get you away from here," she said and tried to pick Enora back up.

Enora shook her head and took a step back.

"No way, I have to help them. I need…" Her words dried up fast as a Vampire rounded the corner, blood dripping down its face.

"Get out of here, Shifter, all I want is the girl," the Vampire spat.

Sarah stepped in front of Enora and glared at the Vampire.

"You really want to risk war with the Shifters over a human?"

The Vampire smirked.

"We both know she isn't just human. Step aside," he growled.

Enora tried to move around Sarah. She couldn't let this young girl risk her life to protect her any longer. Enora wasn't helpless; she was weak at the moment, but could muster enough energy to disable a lone Vampire.

"You're right, I'm not just human," she said and raised her hands to blast him with a shot of defensive energy.

He laughed and straightened.

"Do your worst, Aura. I want to know how much power I'll be gaining when I get my hands on you," he said.

Enora wasn't going to fall for that bait. She knew exactly how much energy was needed to knock the Vampire on his ass long enough for her and Sarah to get a safe distance before he could get back on his feet. Still, she couldn't resist an extra little kick to let him know she was more powerful than he bargained for. As soon as the Vampire was toppled, she grabbed Sarah's hand, and they took off down the street.

"I'm glad you came to your senses," Sarah said as they ran.

Enora shot her a glare before shaking her head.

"I am getting you to safety, little girl, and then I am going back to help my people."

"I'm going to ignore the little girl remark, but I can't let you go back. Not without sufficient back up," Sarah said before nudging Enora to make a turn.

Enora followed the girl's lead, and soon, they were in front of a quaint house at the edge of town.

"Welcome to the Pack House," Sarah breathed.

"Why would you risk bringing me here? What if the Vampires followed?"

Sarah shrugged.

"They've already proved they don't care about breaking their truce with the pack in order to get to the Aura. Besides, Tyr will want a firsthand account of everything going on before he moves to help."

"You don't think he will help?"

"I know he will help, but that doesn't mean he won't want to cover his bases in case this grows larger than Langsmith and the Shifter Council gets involved."

Sarah escorted Enora inside. Tyr arrived within minutes of them setting foot in the door.

"Sarah! You are in deep, young lady," he said.

For the first time, Enora saw the girl acting her age. Like a teen being scolded by a parent, and she realized not only had she just been saved by a Shifter, but the adopted daughter of the pack leader.

"You can ground me later or whatever, but right now we have bigger problems. The Vampires are attacking the gate, killing Aura and anyone that gets in their way. Including Shifters," she said.

Tyr's concerned parental stance changed immediately. Even without being a Shifter, Enora felt the urge to kneel before his Alpha energy.

"What?" His roar sounded only half human at that point.

"I need to get back to help my people," Enora spoke.

Tyr turned his gaze on her as if realizing she was there for the first time. He blinked, and after taking a deep breath, shook his head.

"I cannot allow my best friend's pregnant mate to return to a battle. Sarah, escort Enora to the cabin. You and Sequoia will look after her until she can be safely handed to her mate."

Sarah looked ready to protest, but one look from Tyr and she took Enora's arm and pulled her right back out the door. Enora was too stunned by Tyr's confirmation of her pregnancy and the fact that Jaq was apparently his best friend to protest. It took her a moment to get her bearings, but by then, she was already well on her way down a dark woodland trail. She had no idea where she was or how to get back to civilization, and so she was forced to keep moving forward.

"Don't worry, Tyr will handle things, and when it's safe, I will take you back myself," Sarah said as if sensing Enora unease.

"Thank you," Enora muttered.

"No need to thank me. Consider this a favor that I may ask to be returned in some way in the future," Sarah said.

Enora couldn't help but smile. Sarah was definitely a character, but the girl was definitely growing on her.

.....

Mack helped one of the elders hobble toward the gate. After the surge, he and the others started gathering the willing to do a mass evacuation. They were headed toward the gate when someone came running down the path, covered in blood, a crazed expression in their eyes.

"The Vampires," the man gasped before collapsing in front of them.

Before anyone could react, several more ran down the path equally as frightened and bloody as the first. The group split, some moving back toward Magelor, others rushing forward to help the fallen.

Mack could feel the pressure building in his skull, the over-whelming sense of déjà vu as he turned to the low hanging sky.

"Everyone, run, we have to leave now!" He hefted more of the elder's weight onto his shoulders and charged forward.

Running into the thick of a battle with Vampires was stupid, but the alternative was being sucked into oblivion by the darkness. There was just as many people streaming into Ceres as there were those trying to get out. It was chaos. It was madness, it was the end.

"It isn't safe," the elder protested, but Mack pushed forward anyway.

"There are people fighting on the other side. It's not ideal, but a fight can be survived. The fall of Ceres cannot," he reasoned as he put her down and urged her to cross.

The elder's body trembled as she took a deep breath before step-ping through in between people fleeing the Aura world. With every person that entered Ceres, the darker the sky became, the stronger the wind whipped around them. The greater the pull was to the cen-ter of Ceres. A low hum could be heard, like a final death nell.

Screams came from all around. Mack turned and raced back to-ward Magelor. There would be others that needed his help to escape. The purple ring of the gate was already dimming and shrinking, they were on borrowed time, and he couldn't just give up on his people. Not now, not ever.

Half way to Magelor, images of Ruling Three's treachery filled his head. He was paralyzed, caught in the onslaught of all the facts at once. He was forced to concentrate to keep the unwanted images at bay. When he finally shook off the visions, his eyes focused on the most terrifying sight. A black hole had formed where the Balancing Crystal used to be, sucking in all the energy and everything it touched. The darkness had arrived.

The few remaining in Magelor ran in his direction. Even those behind him who had sought the refuge of Ceres from the battle with the Vampires took one look at the approaching darkness and turned right back around. A little girl tripped and fell at his feet. Mack picked her up and took off back toward the gate.

The low hum became a deafening roar as the void sucked in everything its path, toppling buildings and tents, ripping up the cobbled streets of Magelor, sending everything into a spiral of panic and oblivion. Mack made it to the gate and handed the young girl off to another Aura as he ushered them through. Donovan, Farrah, Zazzie, and Hendrex crossed with them, but Disrayan was nowhere to be seen amongst the crowd. Panicked, Mack pushed his way back toward the void. Frantically searching the crowd, he finally spotted her. Just as his vision had shown him. Running for her life, the darkness on her heels. He reached out for her.

"Rye!" he screamed.

She reached out for him too. Their fingers touched briefly before the force of the void pulled her back again. He was losing her. He surged forward, latching onto her arm, and with their combined might, they were able to get back to the gate. It was nearly closed now, barely the size of a playhouse door. He placed one foot through as extra insurance as the last of the Aura were forced onto their hands and knees to crawl through one after the other.

"Go!"

Mack looked up to find Jaq bringing up the rear. He'd created a bubble of energy around them, holding the last shreds of Ceres together with his own energy. Mack hesitated in awe of the power on display. Shaking his head, he forced Disrayan to go through before grabbing onto Jaq and forcing them both back and through the gate.

.....

Jaq's entire body felt like it was being ripped into a million little pieces. He screamed and writhed in pain as multicolored spirals of energy swirled around his body. He was vaguely aware of someone else's screams nearby before everything jolted back into place and his body met with cold concrete. Gasping for breath, the air was filled with anguished screams and angry growls.

He rolled over, coming face to face with the second nightmare of the evening. Before him, the supernatural world was locked in battle. Aura stood forming a shield around the gate, allowing for the safe passage of people escaping the failed sanctuary. At the front of them, Jaq recognized a certain redhead. Beyond the Barrier was a clash of fur, fangs, and supernatural energy. Wolves and big cats pounced and tore into Vampires as Vampires sank their fangs into Aura and Shifter alike. At least the Aura weren't just playing defense this time.

They fought back. Using their energy to set fire to their fallen attackers, ensuring they wouldn't heal and rise again. Protecting their Shifter allies and providing back up when they could. Jaq couldn't lay there and let them fight alone. He drew on what little energy he had left to get to his feet, stumbling to the line of Aura where he joined hands with Molly and the others. The energy merged and in solidarity they expanded the shield that Molly and the others had created. As it crept forward, their enemies turned to ash as soon as it met their flesh.

Their allies were safely encased within the bubble, no damage to them. Jaq didn't know how that was possible, but he didn't dwell on it in the moment. The Vampire attackers noticed as well and began to flee from the energy bubble's reach. Jaq felt Molly's hand growing warmer in his as she drew more of his energy. The bubble of death grew until it reached across the street and surrounded the entirety of the factory.

"I think that's enough," he said as his energy waned once again.

He tried to pull his hand away, but Molly's grip was too tight. He let go of the Aura next to him to spare them from being entirely drained. Molly was harnessing the energy in the same way the Balancing Crystal had before it imploded.

"Molly, you need to let go. You will kill us if you don't," he said, and she turned her head toward him.

Her eyes completely white, her skin glowed with an unnatural light. He felt stripped bare under her otherworldly perusal.

"You have shown yourself worthy." A voice in multiples at once came from her mouth, not hers, and yet, still her.

Her eyes drifted closed, and she began to hum. The vibration of her voice magnified by the energy she expelled seeped into his body, melding with his energy and magnifying it. He felt like a live wire was wrapped around his entire body sending a million joules of energy through every nerve ending until he felt like he would explode into flame. When he felt he couldn't hold on any longer, Molly crumpled to the ground. Freeing him and the others from her hold.

One of Maura's Men rushed to her side, shooting daggers at Jaq as he cradled the unconscious Molly in his arms.

"What did you do to her?" he spat.

Jaq shook his head and ran a hand over his face. He could still feel pricks of energy like static against his skin.

"I should be asking what the hell she did to me," he replied.

Despite the electric feeling running through his body, an eerie calm had settled over the battlefield. With the Vampires dispersed or dead, all that was left before them were the bloody remains of the injured and unfortunate. Jaq was overcome with emotion as he took in the scene. A lone tear ran down his cheek as his brain tried to process everything in front of him. He glanced back at the brick wall where the gate to Ceres had once been. His fingers itched to draw the sacred runes, to see that it had all been a mistake. Maybe Ceres hadn't truly fallen, maybe it had just undergone a reset.

He wasn't the only person with such thoughts. He knew this as the first person stood and walked to the stone walls. They carefully dipped their fingers into the ash and drew the runes with the precision of a master. Nothing happened. The ash remained just that, and the symbols didn't glow, not even a flicker. The artist took a step back before falling to his knees, horrified sobs shaking his body.

Jaq made his way to the man and pulled him from the ground. Wrapping him in his arms, he did his best to comfort him.

"This is all your fault," the man sobbed.

"No, it is all the fault of pride," Jaq replied.

The man pushed from his arms. Anger in his eyes.

"It's your fault!" he screamed.

Jaq shook his head. Those that were still able to stand gathered in a crowd around him.

"If you choose to blame me, that is your prerogative, but the words I will speak now are the truth. I am not, nor will I ever apologize for being vocal about Aura rights. We are a strong and powerful people. We shouldn't hide our true nature, banish ourselves to a half-life in a make-believe world in fear of persecution. We deserve better. I demanded better. What happened to Ceres was inevitable. It was never meant to be a permanent home for our people. It was a sanctuary, a temporary shelter for our people to survive the darkest days."

More of a crowd gathered as Jaq spoke.

"Those dark days have long since passed. It was only fear and complacency that forced our people to this point. We should have reintegrated ages ago. Ceres might still have been a viable sanctuary, if not for the reluctance of the leadership to accept the tides of change. My voice is that of the future, my movement is that of the future. Ceres is no more, and the sooner you all come to realize and accept that, the better for us all."

Jaq didn't wait for anyone to acknowledge his words. He was exhausted, and he only had one person's safety on his mind. Enora. He searched the crowd for her and was thankful she wasn't there. Donovan, Farrah, Zazzie, Hendrex, Disrayan, Mack were present and accounted for. Even Xander, Claude and Tyr were amongst those in the crowd.

Tyr approached him. Placing a hand on Jaq's shoulder, he whispered in his ear,

"Your mate and unborn child are safe with my mate and Sarah. When you are ready, I can escort you to them."

Jaq froze and glared at Tyr.

"Child?"

Tyr frowned.

"You didn't know?"

"Of course, I didn't know!"

"Well then, I suggest you come with me right now."

Jaq ran to his truck and followed Tyr to the Shifter compound. There were actual guards at the end of the drive when they arrived, but Tyr instructed them to let Jaq through. As soon as they reached Tyr's cabin, Jaq was out of his truck and bounding up the stairs. Tyr caught up to him and placed a hand on his chest.

"I get how you feel, but understand you are in my territory and in the presence of my mate and family. You will be a gentleman," he warned.

Jaq nodded as Tyr opened the door to the cabin.

"Coy, we've got additional company," Tyr called out.

Sequoia, Tyr's mate, appeared immediately. Under different circumstances, Jaq would have noted the beauty and grace of Tyr's mate, but at the moment his mind was on only one person. That person sat curled up on Tyr's couch with a steaming cup of tea. She wouldn't even look at him.

"Hey, Sequoia. Thank you for taking care of my mate." Jaq managed that small bit of pleasantries before he strode across the room and grabbed the cup of tea from Enora's hands. He set it on the coffee table before pulling her into his arms and kissing her like it had been a million years since their last. In all honestly, it felt like it had been.

He couldn't stop kissing her once he started. Didn't stop until Sequoia's giggle and Tyr's perturbed grumble broke through his subconscious. He forced himself to pull his lips away from hers and sighed. Turning to Tyr and Sequoia, he pasted on a smile.

"Thank you for your hospitality. If you are ever in need," he began but Tyr held up his hand.

"Just get out of here and be safe about it."

Jaq smirked and lifted Enora into his arms. Grateful she seemed content to go along with it and didn't fight or protest like he knew she wanted.

"We'll meet tomorrow afternoon," Jaq called to Tyr as he got Enora into his car.

"We'll play it by ear," Tyr assured him before waving him off.

Jaq got into his truck, anxious to get Enora safe and alone. It wasn't until they were off Shifter land that he realized he had no idea where was safe and where wasn't. All of The Resistance compounds were compromised. His house, although safe, still harbored Aura refugees. There really was only one place they could go, and he hoped it hadn't been compromised as well.

Enora was suspiciously quiet, but after glancing at her, Jaq realized it was only because she had fallen asleep. Her head rested against the passenger window, her breathing shallow and even. Tiny plumes formed on the cool windows every few seconds as her warm breath came out. She looked so peaceful he didn't want to disturb her. Not even when they pulled up to her condo in downtown Langsmith.

.....

Enora focused on keeping her breathing calm and even. It was stupid to pretend she was sleeping after the night she just had. That they both just had. When Jaq walked through the door of Tyr and Sequoia's cabin, she forced herself not to launch into his arms. To break down in tears of joy that he was okay and had come back to her.

Instead, she'd acted like a mute idiot. Letting him guide her wordlessly to the car. She had been too afraid to speak. Not wanting the entire Langsmith Shifter clan to hear all of her business from a firsthand source. So, she waited until they were safely off Shifter property, only to find she wasn't sure what to say to him at all. Whether to admit her true feelings or curse him out for being so reckless. Then, there was the issue of her being pregnant. How was he going to react to that bit of news? So, instead of talking she'd pretended to fall asleep and gathered her thoughts during the drive.

With the car stopped, she was home but still had no idea how to handle what was surely to be a conversation of a lifetime.

"Enora, love." Jaq's voice was soft and warm.

He touched her shoulder, and she made a mewling noise before faking a yawn and opening her eyes.

"Did I fall asleep?"

He smiled and picked up her hand, brushing a kiss across her knuckles.

"It's been a long day. Let's get you safely inside."

Enora nodded slowly before getting out of his truck. He was out of the vehicle and around to wrap his arm around her waist before she could take more than two steps toward the front door.

"You don't have to do this. I know you have more important things," she began, but Jaq swept her into his arms and kissed her soundly.

"You are what's important right now. Don't ask me to leave you alone tonight because I can't." He carried her up the stairs and used her key to open the front door.

"We need to have a talk, but right now isn't the time," she protested, squirming out of his grasp as soon as they crossed the threshold.

He set her down but didn't let her go. He closed the door and pulled her in for another kiss.

"You're right," he whispered against her lips, "the last thing I want to do right now is talk."

When he kissed her again, Enora didn't fight it. She wanted him too much to deny this final act of intimacy between them. Baby or no baby, Jaq was dangerous for her. Too dangerous to her heart, and her body if tonight was any indication. He courted danger more than he had ever courted her.

"Bedroom," she gasped as he nipped at her exposed collarbone and cupped her breasts with his hands.

Jaq groaned and pulled her shirt over her head before taking her breast into his mouth. Hot and wet through the thin fabric of her lace bra, he suckled her as he carried her up the stairs. She was only vaguely aware of them both continuing to disrobe, but in the end, they were naked by the time he tossed her unceremoniously on the bed.

"What do you want tonight, love?"

Enora moaned as he slid two fingers roughly inside of her, crooking them until they came into contact with her g spot.

"Just fuck me already."

She reached for him, but he dodged her grasp. He pressed his pinky to the puckered flesh of her anus and swirled his thumb over her clit to ease the sting of the intrusion.

"I'm going to fuck you in due time, but I want you to tell me how. How many orgasms do you want? I can promise you two on my dick, but so many more if you want to play first," he said.

From any other man, Enora would assume he was exaggerating his prowess, but with Jaq, she knew he was telling the truth. Part of the reason she'd been so hung up on Jaq was his unnatural ability to give her mind-blowing orgasms like he was passing out Halloween candy. He knew all of her sensitive spots, every button to push, and with just the right amount of speed and pressure. And that was before he slid his dick inside of her. He fit like a fucking glove, filling every inch, every vein perfectly positioned to glide just right over her nerves.

She bit her lip, just the thought of all the things he could do to her was enough to have her teetering on the edge.

"Words, love. I need your words."

Jaq slid his thumb over her clit again, and that was just the push she needed. Her hips raised from the bed, pressing into his hand as he teased her orgasm to great heights and kept it there until it was almost painful. Then he pulled his hands away and sank between her legs, lapping the juices that ran freely from her worked-over flesh.

"Oh, Oh, OH!"

Jaq chuckled at her exclamation. Enora thrashed on the bed, her hands fisting in her sheets as he devoured her. His fingers had been rough, but his tongue was a gentle torment.

"Have I told you how much I love this pussy?"

He spread her folds with his fingers before delving back in with his tongue. Enora could barely breathe as the second orgasm tore through her. He lapped at her until the waves of pleasure subsided before pulling away. Enora lay on the bed, eyes on the ceiling as her body cooled. Jaq went into the bathroom, and she heard the water turn on as he ran a bath and presumably, washed his face and hands. She took the opportunity to take a quick nap while he set his next seduction scene. She knew she would need the extra energy for the night ahead.

When she awoke, it was to Jaq picking her up. Her head resting against his chest, she reveled in the warmth of him. The steady beating of his heart almost lured her back to sleep. He carried her to the bathroom and stepped into the tub, lowering them both into the jasmine scented water. Enora settled on his lap, resisting the urge to wiggle against the length of him pressed between her cheeks. She rested against his chest, letting the water relax her muscles as he lazily ran his hands over her belly under the water.

"I worried about you today," she admitted.

"I worried about you, too." He pressed soft kisses along the back of her neck and shoulders.

"What you did to Maximus was stupid and reckless and..." her words drifted as he shifted his hips so his erection sprang between her legs. Sliding across her sensitive flesh. The head of him poking through the apex of her thighs and rested hot and thick against her.

"No fussing tonight, Enora."

He cupped her breast with his massive hands, thumbing her nipples into stiff peaks. He shifted his hips again, his dick sliding up and down, teasing her into submission. The water sloshed back and forth with his movements, barely contained by the lip of her tub. Enora felt his heart rate pick up as he stroked and fondled her. The snippy reply she came up with was lost as another orgasm washed over her. Another reminder why this would be their last night. She needed her wits about her, which was impossible in his presence. Especially, when he had mastered her sexual being like this.

"Enough," she sighed and tried to pull herself from the water.

Jaq grabbed her hips, pulling her back. Her traitorous body demanded more, hips shifting to slide back on his erection. Her inner muscles clenched around him.

"It will never be enough," he hissed in her ear before his hips began to move again.

The pads of his fingers dug into her thighs as he held her in position. Half squatting, giving him enough room to maintain his punishing pace, Enora gripped the edge of the tub, water sloshing over her fingers and onto the floor. She couldn't care about the mess they were making, her brain fully focused on the slide of his dick, the roughness of his pubic hair against her inner thighs. She knew when his control broke. His movements became stuttering and erratic as he pulled back as far as he could go without leaving her completely before slamming into her. With an almost feral sounding growl, he seated himself deep and his dick pulsed inside her, pressing the very limits of her womb.

His grip on her hips tightened to the point of pain that only

122

heightened the pleasure coursing through her veins. She followed him over the edge, her inner muscles rippling and milking him for everything he had. She fell back against his chest, breaths coming in short gasps.

"What a mess," Enora said after a moment, and Jaq chuckled.

"I'll clean it when I recover enough to get us both out of this tub."

Enora peered over the edge of the tub and shook her head. Water was all the way to the door, but that wasn't the mess she was talking about. She was the mess, he was the mess, they were the mess. She pulled herself from the tub, careful not to slip on the slick wet tiles, and grabbed a towel.

"You do that," she replied, and she couldn't help but hope he did.

Not just the mess on her bathroom floor, but the mess he had made of her life.

.....

Mack waved Shane and Molly off before heading back to help the others figure out their next steps. Disrayan scheduled appointments to get the refugees human paperwork on one end of the factory loading dock. Farrah, next to her, took the names of the dead and the missing. Zazzie was third in the makeshift resource line, providing on the spot counseling for those who were still in too much shock to process what had just happened and needed extra reassurance of their safety.

Donovan guided the people through the line while Hendrex shuffled people into the factory as a temporary shelter until they could be properly settled. Watching his friends and family working like a well-oiled machine in the face of chaos was somewhat reassuring that the Aura weren't in fact doomed.

"We should get going. Our presence here isn't helping with settling your people," Xander said, breaking into Mack's train of thought.

"Maybe not, but they need to see that you are on our side. You helped save them today," Mack said.

Claude chuckled.

"I think that distinction goes to Molly, the Super Freak. It's really scary when she goes off like that," he said.

Claude's mate smacked him in the arm.

"Don't call her a freak. It's not her fault she absorbed Maura's powers."

"She's still fucking scary as hell when she uses it."

"You should be nicer to her to ensure that doesn't happen," Xander's mate said coming up next to them.

In her arms, she held a tiny bundle, a look of longing in her eyes before she handed it off to Mack.

"Take her before I adopt another stray," she said, and Xander pulled her into his arms.

"You have never once said you wanted a family." There was a hint of panic in Xander's voice.

Mack couldn't blame the man for his concern. Turned Vampires couldn't procreate. Cat looked away from Xander, turning her gaze back to the bundle wiggled in Mack's arms. She didn't look happy about being with him.

"If we can't find her parents or any relatives to take her in, she will be put up for adoption," he said.

Xander took one look at his mate and ran a hand over his face, shaking his head.

"If she or any other children have no living relatives, we shall take them in. I cannot deny my mate her heart's desires, and we have plenty of space."

"Let's not make any rash decisions about babies at the mansion. Besides, the Aura are scared of us, as is. There is no way they would allow one of their own to live with us," Claude said.

Mack was grateful that Claude, for once, was a voice of reason. With the issue of the Aura being held by Vampires as blood slaves, no matter Xander and Cat's intentions, the Aura population would not be okay with any of their own being raised by them. At least, not yet. Still, looking at the hurt in Cat's eyes and the frustration in Xander's, Mack decided it best not to add to their stresses that evening.

"Why don't we cross that bridge when we get there? Go home and get some rest. I'm sure we will meet again in the morning to discuss our next steps, and it will be best to have clear, rested minds."

"Right," Xander said and guided Cat away.

Gretchen took a peek at the baby and smiled.

"She is adorable," she said.

Claude snatched Gretchen away with a scowl.

"Don't you go getting ideas. Uncle Claude is fine, but Daddy is a title that has always given me hives," he said.

Gretchen scowled, and Mack could see one of their epic fights beginning, so he chose to walk away before their heated discussion bothered the baby any further.

He headed toward Hendrex with the girl. There had to be someone to watch her for the night, at least. Disrayan caught his eye as he carried the baby over. He hated how shocked she looked, and worse, when the shock morphed to longing. Mack wanted nothing more than to start a family with Disrayan, but they both knew now wasn't the time. They hadn't even agreed to a binding date yet, which of course would be after Donovan and Farrah. Whenever they wanted to get their act together.

Mack handed Hendrex the baby.

"Is anyone missing a young baby?"

Hendrex frowned at the child, seeming even more awkward in holding the infant than Mack had. He walked to Farrah and tried to pass the baby to her, but the quelling look she gave Hendrex had him pulling the baby back. She checked her list and smiled.

"I believe this is young Adora. Her mother broke her arm during the fight and was taken to the hospital. I can have her brought to her on the next run," Farrah said.

Mack and Hendrex both sighed with relief. One problem solved. At least, one mother and baby would be reunited that evening.

Hope

Jaq reluctantly slid out of Enora's bed. She was fast asleep, her naked body splayed in the middle of the bed. There may not have been much talk between them last night, but he knew that he'd made progress with her in the relationship department. Unfortunately, instead of waking her to initiate another round of sex, he was sneaking out in the wee morning hours. The sun was barely above the horizon, and he knew it would be another hour at least before she woke on her own. Maybe longer, given everything she had gone through the night before.

Hell, he wished he could sleep in too, but his phone had begun buzzing precisely at 6am. He'd ignored it the first two times, but when he realized the calls weren't going to stop, he reluctantly answered. Mack let him know they were meeting to discuss what would happen next, both with the Aura and the war that had been started last night.

With a sigh, Jaq went in search of his clothes. They were scattered in a trail all the way back to the living room where it had all begun. Where he and Enora had made the decision that carnal pleasures were more urgent than the emotional understanding that there was something serious between them. Hell, Jaq hadn't even brought up the baby with her. He needed to rectify that soon, but the buzzing of his phone told him he was going to have to wait in that regard.

"About time," Hendrex said when Jaq entered their usual meeting place.

"Cut the man some slack, he only just got cozy with his mate. I'm surprised he came at all," Tyr said.

Jaq pulled up a chair and sat across from Xander. The older Vampire frowned at him.

"You just claimed your mate, and you were able to leave her side so soon?"

Donovan cleared his throat.

"Can we save the mate commentary for after we discuss what the hell happened yesterday?"

"Fine by me. The sooner we finish here, the sooner I can get back to where I'm supposed to be," Jaq said.

"Good, now Jaq, what the hell were you thinking going after Maximus?" Tyr said.

"He attacked my people, was holding Aura hostage. I wasn't going to just sit around and let that Vampire asshole think I would just roll over and take it."

"I get it, but there should have been more planning involved. You could have brought us all in on this."

"You guys had your hands full, and it was my problem to deal with. I honestly didn't expect the bastard to actually be there. I just wanted to make sure he knew we weren't going to take his attacks without retaliation."

"Yet, all you did was cause every Vampire in the area to fall in line with terrorizing the supernatural community," Mack jumped in.

"We don't know that for sure. For all we know, the rogues in town recognized a power vacuum and made a move," Claude added.

"I've been able to get some information about how far this has reached, and I have to agree with Claude. The Vampire Council still doesn't know about Maximus's death. Even a few of the Vampires we were able to capture after the fight hadn't known. They didn't give us much information beyond that, but it seemed they had all been sent into a frenzy because of the first energy surge," Tyr said.

"Speaking of energy surges, how is Molly?"

Claude and Xander exchanged looks before shaking their heads.

"Molly is recovering from the battle. She will be fine come the morning thanks to her Vampire healing," Xander answered.

"Well, she is going to need to train with her Aura energy. We can't risk her massive surges anytime she gets into an altercation," Donovan said.

"I'm already on it. Molly is my friend, as well as her mate Shane. My energy will also help maintain balance in case training goes awry," Mack said.

Jaq nodded before taking note that Greg wasn't among them.

"Where's Greg? I thought he would be here, considering..."

Claude put his hand up.

"Greg left with Carrie. She doesn't want anything to do with us after Molly killed her father, and Greg didn't want her traveling unprotected."

Jaq nodded. He had only met Greg in passing, but the man had seemed like the protective type.

"So, the born Vampire element has left Langsmith. I don't know if that is a good or a bad thing at this point," Tyr said.

"Good," both Xander and Claude said in unison.

The entire table laughed before Hendrex killed the mood with his seriousness.

"I know that as Maura's Men you are not exactly on the best terms with the Vampire Council, but is there any way you could maybe convince them to allow you control over the Langsmith area?"

"They would never go for that, especially not now that Maximus died after openly investigating us. We are hunkering down and making contingency plans in case they decide to try and hunt us again."

"I'm sorry if my actions made things worse for you guys, but you have to understand I was doing what was best," Jaq said.

"We know you did what you needed to do, otherwise, we wouldn't have helped. Now, if you have concluded the Vampire side of things, we must be getting home. We too have mates to return to."

"Yeah, once we have word about the Vampire Council's reaction, we will let you know," Tyr said.

Claude and Xander left, leaving Mack, Hendrex, Donovan, and Tyr at the table. There was a moment of silence before Donovan leaned forward and glared at Jaq.

"I don't care what your motives were. What you did was stupid and reckless. You endangered everyone, and I dare say, caused the rush on Ceres that led to its downfall."

Jaq ran a hand through his hair.

"Look, you don't have to understand what I did or why I did it. What happened to Ceres was inevitable and a moot point now. It's done, it's over. Our focus should be on helping the Aura settle in to their new home," Jaq replied.

"I hate to admit it, but Jaq has a point. I knew Ceres wasn't going to last as a sanctuary for our people. His actions alone did not bring about the downfall. We know who that dubious honor goes to. We are all in new territory here. Our people lack leadership, and I am reluctant to assume the role just because."

"Are you saying you want to hold elections? Now?"

"It's far too dangerous for anything like that. The Vampires would surely attack a gathering so large."

"Not right now. We have a brief window of respite until they attack next. They, like us, will still be scrambling to regroup especially without an established leader."

"We can hold the elections at the factory. Most of the refugees stayed there last night," Donovan suggested.

"I'll have my pack run patrols outside for security if you want," Tyr offered.

"Great, then it's settled. We will have elections this evening. It will give us enough time to alert everyone and give those who are interested in leading a chance to rally support," Hendrex said.

"I still think it's a shitty idea. People are still grieving, still recovering. We need to give this more time."

"Normally, I would agree, but the longer we wait, the more likely we will be scattered and disorganized when the Vampires attack again. We need to be on the same page under new leadership, so when it comes time to talk, we can present a united front."

"I'll let my people know. I gotta get back before Enora wakes," Jaq said and stood to leave.

The tea kettle whistled, signaling Enora that the water for her tea was done. She was wrapped in a big fluffy robe and pouring the boiling water over a cup of black tea when Jaq walked through the front door. She quickly reached for a knife before she realized it was him and not a Vampire intruder.

"Whoa, slow down, Buffy. It's just me," Jaq chuckled closing the distance between them.

She didn't let go of the knife right away. Instead, she kept it firmly in her grasp but flat on the counter.

"I didn't think you were coming back," she said as he grabbed another cup from her cabinet.

"Of course, I came back. I didn't want to leave in the first place," he said.

She let go of the knife and took out another tea bag to drop into his cup before pouring the water over it. He pulled her into his arms and nuzzled her neck.

"I'm pregnant," she breathed, tensing in preparation for his shock, for his denial.

She felt his warm lips curve into a smile.

"I know," he whispered before spinning her around to face him.

"You know?"

"Tyr didn't know you hadn't told me. I'm upset you didn't, but I understand why," he said.

She sighed and touched his cheek.

"I won't keep you from our child, no matter what happens between us," she said.

"Good to know, but I plan to be there for both of you, from this day on. Enora Circinus, will you marry me?"

Jaq sank to his knees before her, fishing in his pocket before producing a blue velvet ring box.

"Jaq! This isn't..." He opened the box and the words dried up in her mouth.

Inside was a rainbow cluster of polished natural stones.

"I know this isn't our custom to propose with a ring, but this is a new day for the Aura, and we deserve a new start with it. If you want a traditional binding, I will go with it, but I am just as happy to take you to the local courthouse and do it the non-traditional way as well."

Enora shook her head, tears rolling down her face.

"I don't know what to say," she admitted.

He smiled and took the ring from the box before sliding it onto her left ring finger.

"Say yes, say yes to a second chance, say yes to us, say yes to a future of love and companionship."

She wiped a tear from her cheek and laughed.

"Who knew you were such a romantic," she said.

Jaq kissed her before letting her go.

"The only person who needs to know that is you."

Enora pulled the tea bags from their almost forgotten cups and used them as an excuse to put space between Jaq and herself as she tossed them in the trash. Jaq picked up his cup and took a careful sip, his eyes following her every move.

"Can I think about it?"

Jaq set his cup down and frowned.

"What is there to think about? We are in love, and you are carrying my child," he said.

Enora blinked slowly and shook her head.

"You never once said the L word before knowing about the baby," she said.

Jaq crossed the room to her. Placing a hand on her cheek, he made her look him in the eye.

"Maybe I would have if you hadn't avoided any serious conversation between us like the damn plague. I love you, Enora. I have always loved you. If there was a shred of doubt in my mind that we weren't meant to be, I would never have pursued you in the first place."

She bit her lip, reveling in the feel of his warmth on her cheek. His brown eyes intense and focused solely on her. She wanted to believe his words. Wanted to believe her feelings weren't one sided. She grabbed the hem of his shirt and pulled him closer. The sexual chemistry crackled between them as they stared into each other's eyes. Enora tentatively reached out with her energy, letting it wrap around his body. He groaned before bringing his lips to hers, just a soft press of warm luscious lips against hers.

She teased the seam of his lips with her tongue, wrapping her energy tighter around him. She taunted him. She knew how he hated sharing energy with anyone. It was a personal and intimate act, but if he wanted her to believe his words were true, he needed to show it. She wasn't demanding a full merge, just a taste. Just a hint of his inner essence and she would know.

"Enora," Jaq warned, his voice gruff and heavy with arousal.

"Do you trust me?"

"Love."

"You expect me to step into a lifelong partnership on words alone. You share your body freely, but there is so much you hide from me."

She slid her hands along the zipper of his jeans before cupping the length of him bulging along his inner thigh. She concentrated her energy there, knowing it would feel like a million butterfly kisses along his flesh.

"You're playing with fire," Jaq growled.

His lids were heavy as he fought his own arousal to maintain eye contact.

"You're playing with my heart," she countered, increasing the energy flow until he shifted his hips away.

"I'm giving you everything you want," he snapped.

"What you think I want."

"Then tell me what you want, Enora. Anything."

She smirked before shedding her pajama pants and hopping on the counter. She crooked a finger at him, and he came to her.

"I need you, all of you."

He nodded slowly before sliding her underwear over her hips and to her ankles.

"As I've been telling you, love. You've had me always and forever," he said before lowering his head to lick her lower lips.

Enora's head fell back as Jaq's energy trailed from his tongue along her engorged flesh. It lingered like tingling sex aid gels, only specifically targeted by Jaq to both heighten her arousal yet keep shy of exploding all over his magic tongue.

"More," she hissed.

His warm breath tickled her inner thigh as he chuckled.

"Anything for you, love," he said.

His tongue dragged firmly against her clit as he said "love" and a jolt of his energy sent her over the edge.

"Fuck!"

She was lost in the sensation of the energy induced orgasm riding her nerves like a pleasure coaster. Up and down and all around, she never wanted it to stop. Her body craved more even as it drew close to short-circuiting from the intensity. She vaguely registered Jaq shifting around to get out of his own clothes. She only knew the absence of his body lessened the effects of his energy on her body, and she didn't like it.

She forced herself up, reaching out for him.

"Easy, love. I'm right here."

He twirled her clit between his thumb and forefinger, and her hips shot up from the counter, greedy for his touch. Her own energy swirled around the room. Encircling them both, but not mingling with Jaq's. She wanted that connection with him but knew she couldn't force it. He needed to make that decision, and she hoped he did. Otherwise, what was happening between them now was nothing more than their usual sexual adventures with an added bonus of energy play.

"More," she cried again.

Jaq bent to take her mouth with his. Their tongues dueled as he positioned himself at her core. She wrapped her legs around his waist, urging him forward, but he held steady.

"You're mine," he growled before sliding into her primed cavern.

Enora couldn't formulate a response as his energy surged forth, connecting with hers at the core of her body. If her orgasm before had been a thrilling roller coaster, this one was the Niagara Falls and Fourth of July of orgasms. Pleasure erupted from every cell in her body and she literally saw the grand finale of fireworks before her eyes.

"I'm yours," she gasped.

White, hot light blocked out everything but the two of them as

Jaq roared out his own release. She could feel him thick and pulsing deep inside her body. Warm jets filling her and spilling from between her legs as he pumped out his release.

"Fuck! If you weren't already pregnant, you damn sure would be after this," Jaq gasped when he was finally able to catch his breath. His voice sounded hoarse from his screaming release, and it filled her with pride to know he'd been so overtaken by her. That they had finally connected in a spiritual way.

"I'm keeping my name," she said after a moment.

Jaq looked up at her, his eyebrow raised in question.

"Huh?"

"When we are bound, I will keep my name."

Jaq smiled and kissed her before frowning.

"My kid will carry the Andromeda name. You don't want to share a name with your child?"

Enora shook her head.

"For someone who loves to push the limits of tradition, I never would have expected you to be so closed-minded about this."

Enora tried to wiggle out from under his body, but he held her fast.

"I don't care if you don't want the Andromeda name. I just feel it's important that we as a family carry the same name."

"That doesn't make any sense. You just said you want the child to have your name and that I should want to have your name too because they will."

"I know what I said."

Enora pushed on his shoulders, and he gave her enough space to get off the counter. He looked like he was going to say more, but his phone began to buzz in his pants pocket on the floor. He cursed and reached for his pants.

"You're seriously going to answer your phone right now?" she hissed.

"With everything that's happened lately, you expect me to ignore it?"

"Take your damn call outside then," she snapped.

The phone stopped ringing. She glared at him. Daring him to leave her for a phone call in the middle of their time together. He took a step toward her, but when the phone began to ring again, he looked at it and frowned.

"I really have to take this call, but our talk isn't over. This isn't over."

Enora threw up her hands and stormed up the stairs. She could hear him answer the phone call as he hopped around getting his clothes back on.

"One step forward, two steps back," she muttered.

.....

Cursing up a storm, Jaq drove to his apartment. The new headquarters until they could ensure their other gathering places were safe from the threat of Vampires. Jasmine had called to ask about next steps, and since it was his duty to take care of them, he was forced to leave Enora sooner than he had liked.

Jaq opened the door to his apartment to chaos. Members of The Resistance were packed into the tiny space, while the teens he'd been harboring huddled in the corner together scared and confused.

"Everybody, listen," Jaq bellowed, slamming the door shut.

The room grew quiet, and all attention zeroed in on him. He took a deep breath and ran his hand over his face. There was no way to sugar coat the news he had to share, so he just jumped right in.

"Ceres has fallen."

There were shocked gasps and anguished sobs as he continued to fill everyone in on what occurred last night.

"So, that's it? We're just supposed to move on?" One of the teens spoke.

"Not just move on, grow as a people. You yourselves came here to forge your own paths. This situation is not ideal, but nothing in life is guaranteed. Ceres was never a guarantee of our safety. No matter what our ancestors intended. It stifled our growth, weakened us. This is a chance to change our destiny. To show the world just who we are. The good and the bad," Jaq said.

"How can you be so cocky after what the Vampires did to us?"

"It's not cocky, it's confident. I, and a handful of others, were able to take one of their leaders. To free an Aura woman who had been enslaved for years. We uncovered the true threat to our people. The one responsible for the death of Ruling One and the enslavement of many more of our own. That threat didn't come from the outside world, and it didn't come from the Vampires. It came from Ruling Three. One of our own. He sold out his people for the promise of power. He stole energy from the Balancing Crystal endangering lives and the stability of the Barrier for vanity sake."

"Those are just rumors," someone said.

"I saw it with my own eyes. Helped to save those that I could. Fought the Vampires who waited on the other side of the gate to ensure their safety. That was my journey. Now it's time for you all to choose yours. The Resistance is on a new path. One to help transition the Aura to a new society outside of Ceres. If that's not what you want to do, then there's the door. If it is, then help me get things back on track. Starting with finding new safe meeting places that aren't my private space. Either way, today is the day we all have the chance to make a major difference in how things move forward. A vote for the Ruling Council is being held this afternoon at the factory. Whoever is chosen can either be an ally to The Resistance or another hurdle for us to jump. I advise you all to vote with your heart and moral compass."

With that, Jaq turned to open the door behind him. He stood there waiting for someone, anyone, to make a move for the door. To take the out he offered, but after several awkward moments, no one had moved.

"Close the door, man. We have some planning to do," Jasmine said.

A chuckle rounded the room. Jaq shook his head and smiled before closing the door.

"Let's hurry this up. I've got shit to do before this vote."

"Yeah, yeah. We heard you're getting locked down. Congratulations by the way."

Jaq shook his head.

"It's not set in stone yet. She's still fighting the inevitable."

Jasmine patted his shoulder.

"I honestly can't blame her. I love you like a brother, but your reputation was well owned."

Jaq shook his head.

"I won't argue that. Now, let's start thinking up new places and/ or ways to ensure the old ones are safe enough to return to."

.....

"Girl! When is the ceremony?" Zazzie gushed as soon as Enora joined her and the others for coffee.

Enora had forgotten all about the ring Jaq had slid on her finger. Too busy mulling over how she was going to get out of her situation with him.

"It's not like that."

"Uh, my brother didn't just give you any old trinket. That, my dear, is a family heirloom. It means everything," Farrah said giving her a pointed look.

Enora groaned and placed her head on the table.

"Why is he doing this to me?"

"You've both obviously been doing it to each other, otherwise that baby wouldn't be in your belly," Disrayan snorted.

Enora tilted her head to glare at her friend.

"Look, he's my brother, so I know he isn't exactly the ideal catch. He's immature and impulsive, totally pigheaded, and to top it all off, he has the Andromeda energy boost to back it up," Farrah said.

"And he's hot, like women faint in his presence hot, and he has never shied away from taking advantage of that. Until recently."

Zazzie added the last part after Farrah shot her a look.

"All of which doesn't matter if you love him, which you do, otherwise it wouldn't have gotten this far in the first place," Disrayan said.

"Ugh, I hate that you are so rational about this when it is anything but rational," Enora said.

"The only thing irrational is you trying to find a way out of what has already happened. You two fell in love and made a fucking baby sharing that love with each other. Now, be a big girl and admit you want nothing more than to join the Andromeda clan. Rye's doing it, Zazzie's well on her way as well," Farrah said.

Zazzie snorted.

"Hendrex and I are just having fun. No binding ceremony is in the works," Zazzie said, earning her an eye roll from everyone at the table.

"You might be having fun. Hendrex has been all in since the moment he got out from under the Ruling Council," Disrayan said.

"Facts," Enora backed her up.

"Like I said, we were all family before, and your romantic involvements will only make that official. Anyway, knowing Jaq, he is pressing for you to be married ASAP, so I give you my blessing to tie the knot before Donovan and I," Farrah said.

Enora shook her head and sighed.

"Not necessary. It isn't happening. I already told Jaq I am not marrying him just because he knocked me up."

"Of course, you're not. You are going to do it because you love him. And yes, that is a fact. I saw it, so save yourself the trouble of fighting the inevitable. Also, our nephew is going to be absolutely adorable."

"Zazzie!" Farrah admonished, but her tone of voice didn't match the huge smile on her face.

Enora stared at Zazzie in shock. Disrayan shook her head and used her perfectly manicured finger to close Enora's gaping mouth.

"Well, with that bit of good news, can we talk about the shenanigans occurring in the next hour?"

All the girls groaned.

"Whose dumb idea was it to hold elections this soon? I mean, it wasn't a great idea before Ceres fell, and it's even worse now," Farrah said.

"You know it was Hendrex. He hates disorder, and with everything going on, the lack of leadership is only going to make things worse," Disrayan said.

"Hey, give Hendrex a break. We all know he is right about that," Zazzie jumped to his defense.

"People need time to grieve, to wrap their heads around their new reality. Voting now is reckless," Enora said.

"Well, they've had me drawing up nomination forms all morning, so at least we know the voting pool will be changed."

"Ugh, please let them keep Hendrex off the Council. I just got him to myself," Zazzie pouted, and Enora rolled her eyes.

"The people removed him because they didn't trust him. I doubt our current situation has eased their worries on that front."

Farrah nodded solemnly.

"New nominations were inevitable. I mean, Ruling One is dead, Ruling Three is a traitor rotting in hell for his crimes, and Ruling Two lost all confidence by running from the Vampires instead of staying to fight for the people. Commander Mars might make the list but he won't accept it," Farrah said.

"I don't even want to guess who else might make the list. I have so many other questions about all of this. I mean, I know it's tradition, but would a Council even work outside of Ceres? There aren't too many qualified candidates with the knowledge of the human world to effectively lead," Enora said.

"Not to mention, we've lost too many key officials and elders, and a lot of necessary documentation was lost with the fall of Ceres. We might not even own the factory any longer if we can't replace the deed," Disrayan said.

"Forget the factory, what about all the new families? They are going to need a lot of hand holding at first, and there just isn't enough help," Zazzie said.

"Don't forget that my brother stupidly killed a born fucking Vampire who happened to also be a Vampire Council Member. We may have won the battle last night, but there will be a dangerous power vacuum in the area until the Vampire Council replaces Maximus. Even then, there is no way they overlook his death and give the Aura a pass," Farrah said.

"Speaking of the Vampires. Did you guys see Molly last night? She is definitely not just a Vampire," Disrayan said with a frown.

"The redhead? Yeah, that was something." Farrah shuddered.

"I apparently missed something," Enora chimed in.

"Right, yeah. The Vampires who helped us raid the monster houses. They came to help when the other Vampires attacked, but they also brought their mates. Molly, the girl we thought Mack was fooling around with, was with them. She is crazy powerful. Like, more than the entire Ruling Council together powerful. She and Jaq merged energies and managed to take out all the Vampires attacking us in seconds," Zazzie said.

Enora bristled.

"Jaq shared his energy with her!"

Enora hated how angry she sounded, but she was too hurt to care. He'd willingly shared his energy with another woman. Something she had been forced to beg and plead with him to do with her. Farrah shook her head and took Enora's hand in hers.

"It was to save the Aura, it wasn't personal," Farrah did her best to explain but Enora wasn't listening.

Her heart was shattered in a million pieces, and she was pissed. She stood from the table and stormed out of the coffee shop. She didn't stop at her friends' worried protests. She was on a mission. She pulled out her phone and text Jaq, asking where he was. He immediately responded that he was at his apartment and sent her the address.

Change

Jaq smiled at his phone as he sent Enora his address followed by a tongue and a peach emoji. Maybe he'd misread her attitude when he'd been forced to leave her earlier. He tucked his phone back into his pocket and rubbed his hands together.

"This plan we have is a good start. You all should go and spread the word about the vote. We want all the Aura to have their voice heard in this one."

Everyone but Jasmine immediately got up and started to gather their things to go. Even the teens who had been crashing at his place had found things to do outside his apartment before the vote.

"Look, I know you aren't really okay with the traditional way of things, but I think you should throw your hat in for a Council position."

"Yeah, no. The Council is ineffectual."

"But it doesn't have to be. If you were on the Council, it would put you in a position to enact the change we both know is needed."

Jaq sighed.

"If I decided to throw my hat in the ring, there is no guarantee I would even be chosen. I'm an enemy of the state, remember?"

Jasmine laughed.

"What state? You saved us all from Ruling Three's bullshit plans. You put yourself on the line to protect them from the Vampire attack. They should worship the ground you walk on."

"I don't want that. I just want the Aura to stop hiding and minimizing their greatness. I don't need some bullshit official title to do that."

She shook her head.

"One day, Jaq. One day soon, you will see that as much as you shirk the title, you are a leader. You always have been."

A knock on his door interrupted their conversation. She smirked and headed for the door.

"I'll leave you alone to your company," she said before pulling the door open to a pissed off Enora. Jasmine scooted past her in the doorway and mouthed "good luck" to him before disappearing down the hall. Enora stormed into his apartment and slammed the door before glaring at him. So much for a last-minute tryst before the vote. Something had set her off more than him leaving her earlier.

"Enora, love. What's wrong?"

Jaq went for concerned and caring. Maybe her mood had nothing to do with him.

"You shared your energy!"

Jaq frowned.

"Of course, I did. That's what you said you wanted."

"Not with me, you asshole. With Molly."

It took a moment for Jaq to realize she was right. During the battle, he'd been forced to share his energy to keep Molly from draining the others. It was completely innocent, but obviously, Enora didn't see it that way.

"It wasn't like how I shared with you. Molly is a siphon like Mack. She was drawing too much power from the others. I had to share mine to keep her from doing harm to them."

Enora continued to glare at him. Then her shoulders slumped, and the water works began. He tried to pull her into his arms, but she fought him off.

"No! This! I can't!" She pulled his ring from her finger and placed it in his hand before taking off for the door.

Jaq couldn't let her leave. Not like this. It was time for them to have more of the talk they'd avoided for so long.

"I'm not giving you up, Enora. I can't. I'm sorry I kept myself guarded during our time together, but those days are over now. I've given myself to you completely. I only ask that you give us a chance. A real chance."

Enora didn't move to leave, but she didn't turn to face him either. She kept her back to him. He could see her shoulders rising and falling with silent sobs. He crossed the distance between them and turned her to face him. He wiped the tears from her cheeks and slid the ring back on her finger.

"I never meant to hurt you. I'm sorry. Enora, please." He got on his knees.

If she needed him to beg, he would. Anything to make her see this wasn't something either of them should walk away from so easily. He placed his head on her belly, letting his energy flow and mingle with hers. She gasped and wrapped her arms around him. Their energy danced and intertwined until Jaq couldn't tell where his began and hers ended. That's when he felt it. The third energy, faint but there, reaching out for theirs. A tiny wisp of energy that wavered with the effort to connect. Jaq reached out for it. Helping the energy connect with theirs.

"Oh!" Enora sank to her knees with Jaq, tears shining in her eyes as they connected with his.

"We're a family. We are meant to be. Don't try and keep us apart now," Jaq whispered.

Enora grabbed his head and pulled him into a kiss.

"Do we have to keep the Andromeda name?"

Jaq's heart nearly exploded with happiness as he shook his head.

"No, we don't. I read about this new trend where modern couples are choosing their own surnames together."

Enora rolled her eyes, but her smile didn't falter.

"We have time to discuss that detail, but if we don't leave soon, we are going to be late for the vote," she said.

Jaq kissed her again.

"Oh, we're going to be late as fuck. No way are we leaving before I make you cum at least three more times."

Enora didn't protest when he guided her to the floor, so he took that as her answer.

"Just make it quick," she gasped as he slid his hand into her pants.

"The first one, sure, but I plan to savor the next two," he growled.

He hadn't sent her the peach and tongue emojis for nothing.

.....

They made it on time for the vote, despite Jaq's multiple attempts to make them late. He wasn't the only one who knew how to push buttons. All it took was getting Jaq a little too worked up and impatient to have him cursing and shaking with his own release. Then she'd gotten him back into his clothes by promising a little deep throat action in the car on the way over.

Nothing got to Jaq like promises of her breaking her good girl persona in a less than private situation. Something she had learned after his visit to her office but hadn't felt comfortable in exploring until now. Enora made a show of wiping her mouth and licking her fingers clean before hopping out of Jaq's truck. His fly was still open, his dick softening is his lap.

She'd toyed with him on the ride over, careful not to distract him from the road, but as soon as he'd parked, she'd given him everything she promised and more. When he didn't make a move to fix himself, Enora tapped on his window.

"Come on, Jaq. You know I hate being late," she admonished.

He groaned and quickly fixed his pants. He trailed behind her until they reached the cafeteria of the factory. It was the only space large enough to comfortably fit everyone and provide a space for nominations and voting to occur. Jaq grabbed her waist and nuzzled her neck as they entered the room. An unnecessary show of possession that would normally get under her skin, but for some reason, she found it endearing now.

"As soon as possible, I'm going to return the favor," he whispered in her ear.

Enora blushed and pulled out of his grasp.

"I'm going to go help Rye. Why don't you find Mack or Donovan or someone?" she said.

Jaq pulled her back and kissed her before letting her go again. "I'll find you later," he said before disappearing into the crowd.

She took a moment to appreciate his taut backside as he walked away before going to help Disrayan distribute and gather nomination sheets.

"Thank the gods! Here," Disrayan handed her a stack of papers, "I need you to make sure that anyone without one of these gets one."

Enora sighed and turned around to face the crowd. Anyone without a nomination sheet, got one, until Jaq was the only one left. He smiled when he saw her and placed a kiss on her cheek when she handed him the nomination form. He had been chatting with a group of men she didn't particularly recognize.

"Thanks, love. Are they going to be collecting these soon?"

"I don't know. I'm sure there will be an announcement," she said and sauntered away.

Her stack of papers was almost gone, but she couldn't find anyone in need of one. Zazzie, who was manning the door, signaled that there wasn't anyone else she could see coming. Enora was equal parts glad and distraught. The number of Aura in attendance was great, but not nearly what she imagined it should have been. She wondered if there were some who hadn't heard about the vote or just hadn't cared to show. She pulled out her phone and loaded the Aura Underground. There were plenty of posts about the vote with all the details about the where and the when. One would have to be living under a rock to not know about the vote. Which meant if anyone was missing, they had either moved too far away to make it on such short notice or honestly didn't care.

Disrayan whispered something to Commander Mars, and he went to the front of the room where a bullhorn was sitting on one of the cafeteria tables. He picked it up and studied it before Donovan came over to help his father work the thing.

"All nomination forms have been passed out. If for some reason you have not received one, please go directly to the Magistrate at the table on the far wall to get one. Nominations sheets will be collected in ten minutes."

Commander Mars set the bullhorn down with a rare smile before his features returned to the familiar, stern old man everyone was used to, and he marched back into the crowd. The room was near silent as people waited for the ten minutes to pass. There were a few hushed conversations about who should be nominated, but from what Enora could hear, everyone was just as on the fence about the vote as she was.

Enora wandered the room catching bits and pieces of conversations. It wasn't just the question of who deserved to be nominated, but what exactly they would be nominating them for.

Why are there so many lines?

Do we seriously need a whole Council?

Why not just let those who want it fight it out first?

One person can't possibly know what's good for everyone.

Well, four somebodies didn't help us out much either.

Why is it only four anyway?

Shouldn't there be a fifth in case of a tie?

Enora was beginning to think they needed more than ten minutes but steadily, the conversations died to be replaced by the sounds of pencil on paper. Enora found a free table space and sat to write her own nominations. There were six lines available. Presumably, for four Council Members, one Commander, since Commander Mars had expressed a need to retire after the battle at the gate, and one for Magistrate.

As far as Enora knew, Disrayan loved her job and had no intention of losing it, but when elections were called because of lack of confidence, her job as Magistrate came up for a vote as well. Honestly, Disrayan was a great Magistrate but her skills could be put to use in a greater capacity. Enora smiled as she wrote Disrayan's name first on the nominations. Next, she wrote in Zazzie because there needed to be someone emotionally in tune with the people on the Council. Donovan was the easy choice for the next Commander, as was Hendrex for the Magistrate position. Despite his objections to leadership, he had the analytical mind and organization to pull off the job. She listed Mack for the third spot on the Council. Not for any real reason, except it would be hilarious if he was voted in because he'd run from his responsibility too long, and karma. That left one final spot on the list.

Enora searched the faces in the room. She didn't know anyone else who would really fit with the Council. She had no idea the strengths of the people around her, so she wrote the only name she knew other than her own. Jaquis Andromeda. A long shot, for sure, not even a serious nomination. He had his place with The Resistance, and the odds of him ever falling in line with the tradition of the Council was slim to none. Still, the idea wasn't too bad the longer she thought about it. Jaq had surprised her in more ways than one recently. Either way, they would all know soon who would have the fate of the Aura and their future in their hands.

.....

Jaq didn't give a damn about this vote. It was a sudden realization as he stared at the nomination sheet in front of him. Not that he thought there wasn't anyone qualified or suited for the job. He just realized how deep his apathy for the whole system had become. The Aura deserved strong leadership, but who's to say they would choose wisely.

He surely couldn't say that. He scribbled in his choices. Disrayan, Donovan for Commander, Mack, Hendrex for Magistrate because making him a Council Member when he obviously loathed the job was too cruel, even for Jaq. That left two more Council spots. Farrah was out of the question, even though it would be hilarious to see the bickering it would spawn between her and Donovan.

There had only ever been one female on the Council at a time, despite most Aura deferring to the women of their families when it came to major decision. So, he wanted to break that tradition. He put Zarovia or Zazzie because she was truly in touch with the people, more specifically, the youth, and would always have their interests in mind. Other than that, he didn't feel right voting for himself, so he put Jasmine, as she was his second for a reason. She could handle the position, and he knew she would do well with working with the others.

As soon as he finished, Commander Mars was back at the bull horn looking like a kid in a candy store as he brought it to his lips. His booming voice on steroids bounced through every inch of the room.

147

"Time to submit your nominations!"

Jaq folded his paper and made his way to the Magistrate table where Disrayan and Enora sat collecting the nominations. He frowned when he realized Enora had chosen the one volunteer position that would make it impossible for him to steal her away for some fun while the nominations were tallied.

Enora winked at him as he handed over his form, and he shook his head. She would pay for her cheekiness later. For now, he would catch up with the guys. Mack, Donovan, and Hendrex were huddled in the corner after handing in their own nominations. They waved him over as soon as they saw him looking in their direction.

"We aren't sharing who we nominated, but we felt the need to discuss what happens if the choices are less than favorable," Mack said.

Jaq snorted. "The same thing I've always done. Fuck the system, man."

Hendrex and Donovan both rolled their eyes at him.

"Look, you can run off with your merry band of misfits if you want, but it won't change the fact that the Vampires aren't done with the Aura, and if we get the wrong leadership in place, it will hinder any chance of us being able to turn this shit pile into an acceptable outcome," Donovan said.

"Look, you're a shoe in for the Commander position, it will be up to you to fix the Vampire situation. The rest of us are just innocent bystanders otherwise," Hendrex said.

"We still have the Super Friends," Mack laughed.

"X-men, it's the X-men," Jaq said.

"Speaking of our alliance. Has anyone spoken to Tyr or the Vampires since our meeting this morning?"

"I stopped by their mansion this morning to let them know the little girl Cat found was back with her mother. They are all pretty much preparing for the other shoe to drop. Molly is still recovering from the battle, so no training can be started until she is on her feet, and Gretchen is making Claude search for her brother and Carrie because they both disappeared after Maximus was killed."

"Do you think Greg and Carrie had anything to do with the attack on The Resistance? I mean, we did kill Carrie's Pops, and Greg seemed a little mated to the girl," Jaq asked.

"I don't know. I trust Greg, but Carrie is a whole other story. I'll keep an ear out with the Vamps to see if Greg makes contact with them soon. He should, since Gretchen is his sister," Mack sighed.

"We'll get to that later. For now, we need to focus on this vote. Did any of you overhear who people were open to voting for?" Hendrex asked.

Jaq shrugged.

"The people who talked to me were more worried about how their families were going to survive the human world than who to vote for. I spent most of my time giving a speed class on human life," Jaq replied.

"No one talks to me directly anymore. Even with Ruling Three's treachery revealed. I think they blame me for the Vampire attack and the fall of Ceres," Hendrex said, rubbing the back of his neck.

"I didn't ask, I was helping Rye pass out the nomination forms," Mack said

"I was helping my dad figure out human tech, so I'm just as out of information as the rest of you. Let's just hope it doesn't take long for the nominations and the vote.

⸱⸱⸱⸱⸱

Enora wiped the sweat from her brow. Who knew pushing papers was such a workout? When she finished with her stack, she handed her tally sheet to Disrayan who added Enora's work to the master list. All in all, there were over thirty nominees. The only person who wouldn't be voted on was the Commander. Everyone had either left that line blank or put Donovan's name in for the position.

At least, the Aura had made the right choice there. Disrayan finished with Enora's paper and started on Zazzie's. It was the last to be turned in and would finalize the nominations. Once Disrayan tallied everything, she handed the paper to Commander Mars. He reviewed the paper and eliminated anyone who didn't meet the criteria to be elected. That meant anyone who was too young or hadn't completed the basic levels of Aura education. Zazzie oversaw that those who completed the basic human education weren't stricken from the list. When that was done, there were ten candidates for the Council, three for Magistrate, and Donovan for Commander. Even though he was the only nomination, a confirmation vote would still be held.

Since Disrayan was on the list for two positions, she had to make a choice. Pursue her nomination for Council Member or stick with the nomination for Magistrate. Enora watched her friend as she analyzed every repercussion of her decision before striking her name from the list of Magistrate nominations. Enora smiled and hugged her friend.

"It's going to be great!"

Disrayan shook her head, the nervousness rolling off her in waves. Commander Mars moved to the front of the room to call the nominees forward.

"For the position of Magistrate, will Hendrex Andromeda and Juris Maelstrom come forward?"

Hendrex and a man Enora had only ever seen in passing moved forward. They were each given a minute to plead their case.

"I am honored by your nomination. If elected, I promise to up-hold the Aura tradition, while also allowing for changes based on our current situation," Hendrex said and stepped back.

Juris stepped forward and puffed out his chest.

"I am a lawyer here in the human world. I spent years learning their customs and laws. If I am elected, I will help bring the Aura out of the dark ages. Tradition had done nothing but fail us. It's time we put our finger on the pulse of things and make drastic changes to ensure our future."

Enora rolled her eyes. Sure, the Aura needed to update things, but throwing away tradition altogether wasn't the answer.

"You have heard them both. It is time to vote," Commander Mars announced.

Everyone lined up and filed through to cast their final vote for Magistrate. Then the votes were tallied by Commander Mars and the assistant Magistrate. No one was more surprised than Juris Maelstrom to hear Hendrex would be the next Magistrate.

"The nominee for Commander of the Security Force is Dono-van Andromeda. Please step forward."

Donovan came to stand next to his father, and he bowed to the crowd.

"I am honored by your faith in me to serve and protect. If confirmed, I promise to help secure our place in this new world."

There was a short round of applause from the crowd, which brought a loud groan from Farrah.

"He's going to be intolerable as a boss," she muttered.

Instead of lining up to vote, Commander Mars asked if there were any objections to Donovan's confirmation. None were had, and so Commander Mars removed the ribbon holding the crest of the Commander and placed it over Donovan's head.

"The people have spoken! Commander Donovan Mars."

Commander Mars beamed from ear to ear as he passed the family torch along. Then he fixed his face and handed Donovan the bullhorn.

"I believe it's your turn to handle this mess," the newly retired Commander said.

Donovan smirked and picked up the paper to read off the next item on the agenda.

"The nominees for Ruling Council are as follows, in no particular order:

Maclovis Andromeda
Wesley Moor
Callum Freeman
Jaquis Andromeda
Farrah Andromeda
Jasmine Hyperion
Disrayan Centaurus
Icarus Eridanus
Zarovia Monoceros

Please come forward and state your case."

Enora was nervous for all of them. So nervous, she had to rush from the room and straight to the bathroom. Her stomach was in so many knots. Once she was able to calm down and emerge from the stall, she was surprised to see Sarah standing there.

"You're sick," the girl said and moved to feel Enora's forehead.

Enora brushed her hand away and smiled weakly.

"It's probably just nerves and morning sickness. Thanks for the concern," Enora said.

Sarah eyed her suspiciously before leaning closer and sniffing her.

"Was there something you wanted to talk about?" Enora prodded.

It was clear Sarah hadn't just happened to be there.

"Just making sure you and your baby are safe. It's what pack members do."

"Pack? I'm Aura," Enora said.

Sarah smiled and gave Enora a hug.

"You smell like home. I don't know how or why, but somehow, we are related," the girl said.

Enora couldn't help but laugh.

"I think your nose may be off. I'm from Ceres."

Sarah shook her head.

"I know it shouldn't be possible. I thought maybe it was connected to Tyr. He considers Jaq family, and as Jaq's mate, you are by extension family. But last night, when I saved you from the Vampires? I could smell in your blood. You are not Shifter, but I am not only Shifter," she said.

Enora's eyes widened.

"You think you may be part Aura?"

Sarah looked away.

"I don't know, maybe. I have always been fascinated by the myths, and after the surge, something changed inside."

Enora took a risk, letting her energy flow out. She placed a hand on Sarah's arm. The connection making it easier for her energy to reach inside. Sure enough, there was the tiniest spark of energy. More than any normal human would have, different than the energy a Shifter produced. Enora gasped and pulled away.

"You're right! The surge must have activated your latent energy," Enora said.

Sarah turned to her with wide eyes.

"So, it's true?"

Enora nodded, and Sarah hugged her again. Enora was afraid

the girl would crush her with her Shifter strength, but she was surprisingly gentle with her. Suddenly, Sarah let her go and looked down the hall in the direction of the cafeteria.

"They're voting, you should go back," she said.

Enora nodded but stopped Sarah from taking off.

"Give me your phone. If you have any questions about being Aura, I want you to call me," Enora said.

Sarah smiled and handed her phone over. Enora entered her number and handed the phone back. Sarah gave her one last hug before taking off down the hall toward the exit. Enora shook her head. She knew Aura didn't always stay close to the gate when they left Ceres, but what were the odds of Shifters mixing with Aura? Her scientific mind started going over all the possibilities for the offspring of such a union. It wasn't impossible, but surely had to be rare.

Enora made her way back to the cafeteria in time, getting in the back of the very long line. It was a lot slower this time considering the number of choices, but Enora already knew who she would be voting for. When it was time for her to vote, she didn't linger or make a big deal about it. She wrote the four names of those she thought best suited for the job and went to join Hendrex to wait on the fate of their friends.

......

Jaq looked for Enora in the crowd as he gave his speech, but he couldn't spot her. Not being able to see her face added to his nervousness. Sweat pooled under his arms and along the back of his shirt. He was glad the dark fabric wouldn't show his obvious flop sweat. He'd never been this nervous before. Then again, he had never imagined being in the running for the Ruling Council.

His nerves eased a bit as the crowd lined up for the final vote and Enora slipped back into the room and joined the end of the line. Part of him wondered where she had disappeared to for so long, but he was once again distracted by an Aura male patting his shoulder.

"I know you will make a great leader," the man said.

Jaq smiled and nodded at the man, unsure of what to say. The man moved on before he could reply. He wanted to go to Enora, but he was stuck at the front of the room with the other nominees until the voting was done. The line moved at a snail's pace as people took their sweet time casting their votes. Dinner would be served after the votes were counted. Farrah's favorite Italian restaurant had agreed to cater the event.

The smell of marinara and melted cheese already assaulted his nose and made his stomach grumbled. He realized he hadn't eaten anything all day. No wonder he was so out of sorts, between the physical and emotional gymnastics of last night and today, combined with a lack of eating, Jaq was surprised he was still standing.

Enora was one of the last to cast her vote, and she went to stand next to Hendrex. Commander Mars and the assistant Magistrate counted the ballots. Every minute felt like an hour. Beads of sweat formed on Jaq's brow, and he clenched and unclenched his hands at his sides to keep them from shaking.

"If I'm voted onto the Council, the first thing I am doing is modernizing the damn election system," Farrah grumbled beside him.

Disrayan nudged her with her elbow and glared at her. Jaq couldn't help but chuckle.

"I'm right there with you. Also, term limits. I'm not feeling this lifetime service bit," he replied.

Callum scowled at him and shook his head.

"Like you even have a chance," he said.

Jaq frowned at the man but bit his tongue when he noticed their conversation turning heads. Now was not the time to show anything less than a united front. If Jaq did get on the Council with the guy, they would have to work together to choose the best course of action for the Aura. He smiled at the crowd and went back to staring at Enora. She was the only one deserving of his full attention anyway.

"Attention! The votes have been counted," Donovan announced.

Retired Commander Mars handed him a sheet of paper, and Donovan's eyebrows went up a good three inches.

"You sure this is right?" Donovan's whisper was too incredulous to be soft spoken.

The retired Commander scowled at Donovan and snatched the

paper and the bullhorn from him.

"I am proud to announce the new Ruling Council. The list will be read in the order of most votes, and the person will receive the corresponding title on the Council.

Disrayan Centaurus, Ruling One
Jasmine Hyperion, Ruling Two
Icarus Eridanus, Ruling Three
and
Jaquis Andromeda, Ruling Four.

The crowd gasped, some cheered, others sneered. A definite mixed bag of emotions went through the room.

"Congratulations, bro," Farrah said, giving Jaq a hug after she'd congratulated Disrayan.

He gave her a hug back but didn't linger. He made his way through the crowd, headed straight for Enora.

She smiled and jumped into his arms.

"Don't make me regret voting for you," she said when he finally let her up for air.

"No regrets, love," he promised and signaled to Hendrex that it was time.

She didn't know it yet, but with Hendrex as the new Magistrate and almost the entire Aura population present, he hadn't been able to resist asking Hendrex to perform a Binding ceremony for them once everything was said and done. Within minutes, their friends and family gathered around them. Enora was still none the wiser until Hendrex stood beside them and cleared his throat.

"Jaquis Andromeda!" Enora chastised him, but nothing could wipe the smile from his face.

"I told you we would be wed today," he chuckled.

Farrah presented the cordage that would be used to bind them, and the ceremony began.

Epilogue

Sarah stood just inside the doorway of the cafeteria. She knew she should have left, but now she was glad she had stayed. Watching from afar as Jaq and Enora were bound together. Aura traditions were so weird and fascinating. Sarah couldn't wait to learn more about this side of herself. She was so caught up in watching the happy couple she hadn't realized she had emerged from the shadows by the door. As if drawn like a moth to flame, their happiness and love was so inviting. She forgot she wasn't part of their world. At least, not yet.

"Hey, I've never seen you before? What clan are you with?"

Sarah hissed and jumped back from the man who had intruded on her private thoughts. Her head swiveled frantically as she realized she wasn't by the door anymore but nearly in the center of the crowd. Panicking, she immediately shifted into her cat form and ran from the room. Scared screams and angry shouts rose in her wake.

She didn't stop running until she was safe at the Shifter house on the edge of town.

"Somebody's in trouble," Reign said coming through the front door.

Sarah shifted back to human form and frowned at the man.

"I thought you were in seclusion? Doesn't that usually last more than a week?"

He frowned at her and shook his head.

"I'm still in seclusion, but with everything that's happened recently, I can't just hide out in a cabin. I had to at least let you guys know I was okay."

Sarah nodded, and he strode passed her. She didn't mean to sniff him, but his scent was so much different than before.

"You're not in seclusion! You're mated!"

Reign froze and whirled around.

"What did you just say?"

"I said you are mated. I can smell her on you." Sarah took another sniff of the air around him, "And she's not Shifter, she's..." Sarah took a moment to sort out the smells. She couldn't be sure the energy she sensed wasn't just lingering from being around all those Aura before. Yet, the stench of death was sharp and burned her nostrils.

"Vampire!" Sarah hissed.

Reign growled deep in his throat.

"She had nothing to do with what happened!"

Reign was mated alright. Sarah hadn't threatened his mate, whoever she was, but just the tone of voice she'd used when she said Vampire was enough to trigger his wolf's protective streak. Sarah's cat bristled, her skin prickling with the urge to change and protect herself. To reinforce the pack hierarchy that placed her well above Reign. Not only because of her status as Tyr's adopted cub, but also amongst the spy ranks. Sarah may still be too young to challenge for an official standing in the Shifter community, but that didn't mean she didn't already carry herself as other Shifter youth did.

They stared each other down for several long minutes before the back door slammed shut and Tyr's anger preceded his entrance into the hallway.

"Sarah!"

"Shit!"

"I will tell the Alpha about my mate when it is time," Reign said, and slipped out the back door before Tyr came around the corner.

"Before you say anything. I was just doing my job. I know that Ceres has fallen, but there is still so much to learn about the Aura," she began, but Tyr held up his hand.

"I know I have let you run wild all these years, but the situation now is different. I am removing you from your duties starting immediately," Tyr said.

"What? You can't do that!"

Tyr glared at her.

"I am Alpha here. You will do as I command. From hence forth, you will conduct yourself as the other Shifter youth until your eighteenth birthday," he growled.

Sarah crossed her arms over her chest and let out a frustrated huff. She would fight his edict more but knew that once he pulled the Alpha card, there was nothing she could do that wouldn't risk undermining his leadership.

"Fine," she grumbled but didn't look away from him.

She may be willing to submit, but her cat refused to let her do so completely. They held each other's gaze for a few minutes before she finally looked away. Tyr sighed and crossed the room to her, pulling her into a hug. Sarah stiffened at the contact. Even after all these years, physical contact made her uncomfortable. Thankfully, Tyr recovered from his bout of emotion and released her quickly.

"Please, no more sneaking out. Sequoia can't handle the stress any more than I can," he said with a pointed look.

"I will go see her now, but I'm sure you want to know what I found out while I was out," she teased.

Tyr smiled and nodded.

"After dinner."

About the Author

Stella Williams is a blogger and romance author who lives in Washington state. She has a degree in Anthropology from The University of California, Santa Cruz. Stella prides herself in using her studies to create diverse worlds and characters for her novels. You can find more about Stella on her website

www.serpentinecreative.com.

Keep up to date with Stella Williams and her latest projects.

<u>Join Our Mailing List</u>

https://mailchi.mp/2637cc1d4d12/getcreative

Stella's Catalogue

Maura's Men Trilogy

Xander's Claim

Claude's Conquest

Shane's Redemption

Maura's Men: A Vampire Romance Trilogy

Langsmith Shifters

Coy Wolf

A Night Divine

Bird of Prey

Secret of Ceres

Ferocious

Dauntless

Earnest

www.ingramcontent.com/pod-product-compliance
Lightning Source LLC
Chambersburg PA
CBHW021159110726
47900CB00002B/654